MAN IS MOVING
BEYOND SICKNESS

MAN IS MOVING BEYOND SICKNESS

Tools for Transformation

Aldo Privileggi

authorHOUSE®

AuthorHouse™ UK Ltd.
1663 Liberty Drive
Bloomington, IN 47403 USA
www.authorhouse.co.uk
Phone: 0800.197.4150

Published by AuthorHouse   04/15/2014

ISBN: 978-1-4969-7784-7 (sc)
ISBN: 978-1-4969-7782-3 (hc)
ISBN: 978-1-4969-7783-0 (e)

Contents

Preface

Can you imagine a world where there is no sickness, no pain, no hospitals, no doctors, and no medicine needed . . . ! Is this a possibility?

Mankind is on the forefront and threshold of a new level of conscious understanding, awareness, evolution and knowledge for the first time in modern history. The collective consciousness of this planet is rising and elevating into a higher resonances and vibration simultaneously creating the collective planetary awareness to lift into new frequencies. Because everything in existence is made of frequency or vibration then this maybe the conclusion and completion of an era of time in the evolution of mankind and the dawning of a new one. Furthermore it is a time that we are incredibly fortunate to be a part of and witnessing. This may sound a little unsettling to some as we humans have never really been that excepting toward change very easily. However, not to be viewed as a negative on the contrary it is the beginning of many exciting and fantastic experiences and opportunities that we are going to be a part of. One of the by-products of this transformation is that man will begin to re-member and re-inherit his/her lost capabilities & talents which will enable mankind to move into new levels, new realms, new ideas, new concepts and even beyond sickness. Some of us are already experiencing being able to subconsciously detect the subtle scent of these abilities as they are arising as we move forward and have access to our previously hidden or suppressed innate abilities. We are on the threshold of new ways of communicating within ourselves and each other.

My own experience spending more than thirty years practising meditation and working as a professional hypnotherapist in time line past and future regression therapy and Chinese energetic healing I have been able to raise my conscious awareness to higher levels and receive glimpses ahead of time of the fascinating process that Humankind is in trajectory for is I had a very strong vision a few years back that at the time seemed a little whimsical, however i have began to notice that the things that i saw in the vision are now beginning to manifest and thus i have had to re-visit this vision with more conviction which i now belief is going to happen and can tell you that what lies ahead for us is very exciting.

This is a book of tools for assisting people who would like to raise their vibration/resonance or frequency and consciousness to higher levels of clarity and health so that they can begin to align with the new wave of consciousness that is now becoming more accessible and more available to us. This will assist in perpetuating the momentum of moving into new levels of awareness and clarity which will positively benefit so many areas of our lives such as: health & well being, wealth, individual & collective relationships, and so much more. Many of our previous misinterpreted limitations will be revealed, begin crumbling and dissolve opening up our conscious awareness to new perceptions, new thinking, new feelings, ideas, concepts, lifestyles and greater opportunities.

Acknowledgements

Thanks to my Mom & Dad, Kenny D and Barbie Deakin for being amazing people in my life, thanks to Karen Kelly, Marie, Sarina & Alan Cashmore who although I don't see often enough I love you very much.

Thank you also to Julian Ray, Suzie Mac Lennan, Nevo Yatom, Mark Love, Ama Lia Way Ching, AYC Pure Yoga, Dan (abundance) Moon, for their support
And friendship.

Many thanks to Dr Kam Yuen, Dolores Canon, Barry Deakin.
Darryl Ankh, Gerald Kein, for being great friends & inspiration.

"Thank you to Denise Pontak PHOTOGRAPHY"

"Accepting flow as your friend"

Accepting flow as your friend can have a profound effect on your approach to living and lubricating the negotiating process of change in our lives to produce change that works to your advantage and for you.The art of negotiating change with oneself is actually a natural ability that has been kind of overlooked really almost to the point of total annihilation. I will share with you some of the factore and reason involved with why this has happened but more importantly by learning why this has happened, you gain the opportunity to regain one or more of your most powerful assets and tools for manifesting powerful positive changed work and feelings into your life. Things such as:, re-stored confidence, satisfying relationships, control, happiness and even the overlooked art of neutrality into your life.

Ultimately, all that we want in life is to be happy and abundant. One way of defining abundance is, as Bashar Quotes, *"the ability to do what you want to do, when you need to do it".*

It is my sincere intent to write this book to offer my knowledge to help give you some clarity and deeper insight into bringing you closer to yourself and your infinite potential so that you may learn to enjoy more of what you are capable of doing in your own unique way that brings you fulfilment and happiness. Thank you for reading this book and i hope you can take something of value from it.

About the Author

My name is Aldo Privileggi, I am a licensed, Clinical Hypnotherapist and Hypnotist having been trained in classical, modern, and quantum healing hypnosis. My field of expertise and interest is predominantly in the relationship of the conscious & subconscious mind and power of our subconscious mind. I am particularly experience and interested in the time track future/past life regression work.(past-life regression). I'm also trained and certified in levels 1,2 &3 Yuen Method Chinese Broad-Spectrum Energetic Healing since 2009. I currently reside in Hong Kong SINCE 2005 where i have my ALDO-HYPNOSIS hypnotherapy practice.

The discoveries I have made whilst working with hypnosis and hypnotherapy have been a continual encouraged and strong urge to delve deeper and further into this fascinating field of therapy that is organic in nature and thus continually expanding, growing, and evolving. During the early stages of this therapy work and exploration, it was known more fondly and colloquially as "change work" for the most part. "Change work" is a term that refers to creating new rapid and wanted changes in people's lives and health by helping to bring understanding and clarity their feelings, thought, attitudes, and beliefs about themselves and their environment.

By changing our belief systems, we can change our lives very rapidly and many accession in an instant. We have the ability and can release any negative limitations that we choose to. But most of us don't know how. Usually these negative limitations and beliefs are things that we have picked up along the way from our birth (and sometimes even prior to birth) through to maturity and these beliefs and this knowledge into our lives for various reasons. However, more often than not these belief systems do not originate from within us they are what are known has second hand knowledge and conditioning beliefs and really do not belong to us. Once an understanding of this becomes apparent the obvious question then arises—how to release and undo these limiting beliefs and thus then their limitations and of course dissolve them for good. This can become a new way of living, a lifestyle and becomes a creative and artistic process that can be enjoyed. The more we allow this intergration to take place in our lives we begin to enjoy this process of accessing our hidden potentials and tap into the power that we have. Then life becomes very exciting When we feel like we have some control and most people want to have control over their lives, or at least feel they have control. Even if we say we don't want to have control in our lives, that statement in itself is indicating that we are controlling.

From observations of my clients and my own life I have come to realise that if people could easily make changes or improvements within themselves, certain inner qualities become illuminated which affects self-esteem, confidence, security, certainty attitudes and self-belief, this all escalate. Generally, if people do not know how to make these changes, i have recognised a tendency to form unconscious habits, a sense of denial or apathy can be held towards these areas. This is an unhealthy choice/action to take and leads to mental, emotional, and physical imbalances. If this is not rectified, it will further deteriorate into illness. I have been applying these processes and methods of change with my clients, friends, family and in my own life with great success Overcoming illnesses and financial despair, mending relationships, and creating positive results in many other areas have been the result.

We are all unique, original people/beings here and have different learning experience, perception and stories to explore and share. The beauty is that you are the author of your story. We are all at different learning stations or levels of conscious evolution in our lives, but somehow momentum moves us forward as one, together. There is a natural intergrative collective that urges us to move together in a certain direction towards expansion and if we don't flow with this it creates resistance in our lives and resistance creates tension and stress.

Introduction

I utilise principles of life that have been serving me well, and I would like to share some of these with you and if you find that theses resonate with you please feel free to use them. Sometimes i may be just one sentence or paragraph in a whole book that resonates with you and sometimes thats all you may need at that particular moment to give you the inspiration or momentum to the next level.

First & foremost through my experience with working in the Hypnotherapy and healing fienld for some time now I came to the understanding and believe that well being is our natural default state of well being and that this pervades and reflects back to us in the well-being that surrounds us. Although it appears invisible to the physical eye (just as gravity is), I believe it is the dominant natural principle and default natural state of being in my life. And because I believe it to be a dominant force and a default state of being, I am thus more aware of it and prone to see it, look for it, focus upon it, and entertain it everywhere I observe. Thus, because I am aware of it and look for it, I find it; and as I find it and focus upon it, I am practising igniting the vibration of it until it is inevitable that it finds and reflects back to me again in a cyclic nature.

Therfore I live in a world of well-being predominantly because well-being is what I look for. Every day, in every way, it is my subconscious mind's dominant intent and i practice to focus on what I *want* to see and feel. Every time I find what I want to see and place my attention upon it, I automatically practise the vibration of that, creating and filling my world with the things that I want. Once the momentum of this is set into my subconscious it moves through me as an effortless processes. It takes inertia and some effort for a Aircraft to lift of the runway, however, once it has reached a certain altitude it requires minimal effort to maintain the trajectory.

This then may raise the question about the things that I don't want to see and the relatedness. Of course, I live in the real world, just like you, and from time to time I see things that I would rather not see. But I have realised that I have a choice and I can focus upon the things that I like and that make me feel good or the things that I don't like and that make me feel bad. We cannot consciously focus upon two things at the same time. Knowing full well that focusing my attention on something I want makes me feel good and perpetuates this good feeling, and vice versa, makes this choice clear and attractive. Also, the ability i have to know that withdrawing attention from an object or area diminishes focus on that object or area certainly helps. Dont get me wrong, i still have my ups & downs in life but now my ups & downs no longer have me.

So, through a little bit of practice and trial & error, I have learnt to shift my attention off what I don't want and place it onto what I do want as quickly as possible. As soon as i become aware that i am feeling less than comfortable in any situation, circumstance or event i can immediately utilise this signal to acknowledge this situation and then shift my attention/focus onto anarea that pleases me. In the beginning this becomes a conscious effort, but after a while the subconscious mind begins to understand the idea and behaviour and intergrates it into a natural behaviour to work with and for us.

We are living creative beings and we are creating and designing our lives, every second, minute, hour and day nonstop, 24/7. The problem is that most people are not aware of this amazing principle and opportunity they do not agree with this statement. I often hear people respond to this by saying something along the lines of—if I create my life, then why would I create this life of struggle and frustration I am living?

This incredibly simple but powerful principal, the art of learning and cultivating how to create more "*consciously*" in my life and getting my attention off what I don't want and placing it onto what I do want as quickly as possible has opened up new endless possibilities to create a world of adventure, excitement, and endless possibilities to explore in my life in so many ways. Every day I am excited to see what will be discovered next as i explore this deeper, pushing the boundaries and testing how far it can go. It is exciting for me because, as I am tuning in to a frequency/resonance place in my beingness where good-feeling things can find me and my life then reciporicates by showing me the results getting better and better to reconfirm what im doing is working. This sets up a positive strong feedback loop. In this book I will attempt to share how i have managed this and how this can be achieved by you if its something you would like to experience, and I know with absolute certainty that any person can do this, the only tool that you require is a functioning imagination and you can achieve this, and more as well. It really is a case where the only limits are the limits of your imagination to take you where you want to go.

First of all, let me give you a little bit of background on my upbringing and character. I was born in the UK, and I completed part of my education there in Birmingham U.K. My parents emigrated to Australia when I was twelve years of age. I then continued my seconday education until age fifteen, and then went to I didn't really care too much for the school education system and what it provided in terms of Stimulation. My favourite parts of school were sports. I just coasted through school; passing all of my subjects, but I did so with little enthusiasm.

My real discipline and passion lay in martial arts. I began learning kung fu at age nine in the UK, taking private lessons from my uncle Alan, a belck belt in Kung Fu. When my family and I emigrated to Australia, there were not any kung fu schools locally available, so I began to study & learn karate. I took it very seriously as it was something that excited me at the time, training passionately every day was something i liked. I reached my black belt by the time I was thirteen years old and continued my training into my early twenties. I took part in many competitions and tournaments and still have a few trophies floating around my Mom's Place somewhere. I also studied and trained in Korean Tae Kwon do, achieving a red belt, and trained in some other various styles and forms of martial arts during this period.

At age nineteen, something very interesting occurred in my life that was unexpected and changed the course of my life. One Day after training I was introduced to a person who later became a good friend; he was also martial artist training in a style called Silat, a lethal martial art established in India. He had been conscientiously studying d ifferent forms of meditation and delved quite deeply into it. Up until this point, although i was aware of meditation I had not had any previous meditation experience, but I was open to it and quite curious about it.

We entered into many conversations about this topic and i began to develop an insatiable thirst to know more about this subject matter, and I asked my new friend a lot of questions about it. During every moment we spent together i would milk his mind bombarding him with lot of questions., I found myself naturally focused upon asking questions and finding out more and more information. The more I learned, the more interested it became and the more interested i got. Some days we would talk for many hours daily, and every time we met, this was the topic and all I wanted to talk about.

So seeing my interest and enthusiasum he began to show me a few energy tricks, but to begin with, he taught me a few basic simple meditation focusing techniques, which I began to practise daily.

Nothing significant happened for the first three months or so of practising meditation techniques, except I must admit I was feeling more relaxed and was able to sit quietly and still probably for the first time in my life. I noticed my ability to focus became stronger as well, and through this new opening of perception I realised the contrast and was able to distinguish my current state of being and my previous unsettled and unfocused state of mind and being. Previously my mind was pretty active and was accustomed to jumping around a bit from one topic to another and from this to that. In retrospect this recognition of my restless mind brought me to a further realisation that most of what I had achieved in my life up until that point could have been much more rapidly attained if I had known how to focus in this new found fashion.

One day, however, an unexpected thing happened. I was sitting in a room, just practising my relaxation techniques as I usually did whenever

I had a moment to spare (I would practise even if I had my eyes open and was waiting for something, like being in a que, or traffic etc), I saw two people walk in from opposite sides of a large room similar to a lobby area. As they walked in, they spotted each other and recognised one another immediately. As that happened, they both (im assuming subconsciously) released an energy flow toward each other. I could actually see the column of energy and energy flow travelling from one person to the other person directly across the room. It looked like a tube around the size of one metre in diameter; it was sort of misty clear white color with a kind of steamy appearance. One energy tube was released from one person on one side of the room, and another energy tube was released from the other person on the other side of the room. These two energy tubes travelled and connected to the bodies of each person opposite each other. As they did that, i noticed their auric energy fields expanded and filled with energy at the same time. They were obviously pleased to see each other because i could read the body language. Interestingly however, they were completely unaware and unconscious of seeing the energy exchange that I could see. Undoubtedly, though, they felt the energy exchange that was clear to see by each other response. I realised at this point this kind of phenomenon must occur with everybody when two people meet and connect. But how was it that i had never noticed this before but i now i could?! We are not usually able to see the actual energy exchange between people . . . or are we?. I had never seen this before; it was very interesting and opened up access to new realms for me. This was the first of many interesting things that began to occur and manifest more frequently from that point forward. Soon after that I began to see people's auric fields more regularly and clearly.Later as i became more accustomed to this natural phenomena I was able to distinguish and discern the satus of people's general health, i could see if they were in good health or not, even if I had not spoken with them or even met them before.

The next thing that occurred was that I began to recognise the ability to create things in my life. I would just think thinking about something randomly without any expectation (similar to a fleeting or passing thought). Then i would notice it would manifest into my life soon after. I would think about something, and then shortly after, it would manifest into my life, this became fun and a new game for me. Of course this became very exciting and very interesting, and I was certain, i knew that these changes could have only occurred because I had been practising meditation.

From this point forward i knew there was something more to meditation and life that i had not known about before and my interest in meditation and metaphysics became a new passion.I did not know at the time that this would be a path leading to the very interesting, unfolding journey that it as led to upto now. I have since devoted the past twenty years to the study of the subconscious mind and energy work and; this is the area that has remained of particular interest, passion for me.

CHAPTER 1

Mind Basics

Let's begin the first chapter with a discussion on the working and foundation of the mind—not so much the physical mind, or brain, but rather the brain's energetic presence and influence.

The mind, for the ease of simplicity and explanation, can be separated into two distinct compartments. I'm not interested in focusing so much on the anatomy of the mind, and this is not the purpose of this book. There are many other books you can find that can be of assistance if you're interested in going down that path. The intention here is to increase our *abilities* with an understanding of how the mind works so that you can practice these principles and put them to use to serve you and others. Thus I will purposely avoid discussing any portion of the anatomy of the mind unless it is essential to clarify a related area or concept for further ease of understanding.

Instead, the focus we will guiding you more to engage in a direct experiential understanding of the *how's* of the mind rather than the *why's* of the mind. Ultimatly, we want to learn about the mind's power to learn to make it become our companion and best friend instead of the contrary our worst enemy, which for most people it is. The whole concept here is that we want the mind to work for us with ease.

The two parts of the mind that we are most interested in and need to understand in order to receive the mind's benefits are closely related yet definitely different. First and foremost, we need to distinguish clearly here *that we are not our minds*; our minds are just tools. If this seems a little difficult to grasp, maybe you can just keep an open mind for now and make your decisions and conclusions later. If you can manage to just keep an open mind, this will be very beneficial for you. As the information in the following chapters unfolds for you, you will begin to realise and notice this knowledge for yourself.

Okay, so let's return now to the two portions of the mind that we use consistently & constantly. One part is called the conscious mind, and the other part is called the subconscious mind. Most people think that we use the conscious mind more than the subconscious and furthermore that the conscious mind is the most powerful portion of the two minds. Just to give you an idea, here are a few scientific statistics to help place this into a bit more of a realistic perspective.

For stareters, did you know the conscious mind is responsible for only approximately one-sixth (less than 10 per cent) of the brain's thinking and power and the subconscious mind is responsible for five-sixths (approximately 90 per cent) of our abilities, creativity, and thinking power? The mind, in its totality—meaning the combination of the conscious and subconscious together has the ability and possesses the know-how to solve any problem or situation that we have experienced and is also able to find the exact information or solution needed in any situation or circumstance and provide the guidance, direction, and steps through which this can be achieved.

The following was published in *Psychological Review* in 1956 by cognitive psychologist George A. Miller of Princeton University's Department of Psychology:

> *It is often interpreted to argue that the number of objects an average human can hold in <u>working memory</u> is 7 plus or minus 2. Thus then we can see that the conscious mind holds only about 7 pieces of information in short-term memory. Your subconscious mind, however, stores all the knowledge, memories you have ever acquired along your whole time track. Everything you have ever read, heard,*

read, smelled, felt, thought or imagined, in fact everything that you have ever perceived through any of your six senses is held and stored within this Subconscious part of your immense memory and can even be recalled.

➢ Paying Attention to Our Environment

As we grow up and mature as people, we may begin to see or notice, (if we are paying attention and are aware to the world around us), that there are certain patterns and behaviours subtly quietly working in synchrony and in flux flowing throughout the core of our lives. One of those more obvious subtle patterns is the observation or realisation that some people/ individuals seem to do better than others. We may find or notice that some people do very well for themselves and are generally happy with their dispositions and their endeavours in life, whilst other individuals appear to struggle and are far less fortunate in their dispositions and endeavours. Why does this happen?

We can divide these two types of people into separate categories. We can then analyse and break down the information associated with these differences more clearly to reveal the keys and underlying subconscious behaviours that are responsible for either successful outcomes or unwanted outcomes. Some people would simply label these as wins or losses—in this case, as people who win and people who lose, or winners and losers. I am not fond of the terms "winner" and "loser", so I would like to refer to the winners as group A and the losers as group B.

Group A consists of people who create and manifest results that work and enhance their lives.

Group B consists of people who create and manifest less-than-desirable results for themselves (in other words, results that do *not* work to enhance well-being, positive production, or expansion into their lives).

Have you ever noticed that the people who are doing well also seem to consistently get all the good luck? Not only that, but they also nearly always find themselves in the right places at the right time and meet the right people, attract great relationships, snatch that bargain, make it just in time for the sale, and get all the green lights while driving.

To the group B people who are struggling, it can be very annoying to see others so effortlessly, even nonchalantly, create all of this success and these wonderful opportunities in a relaxed and almost effortless manner. It is true that luck does favour the prepared. However, let's pause. Suspend that notion for a moment and start to uncover the way this happens so we can reveal the deeper essence. Once we can understand the connection and go to the source of what is producing these positive results, we will then have a tool to experience this effortless positive change in our lives. And the more we have, the more we have to share, and sharing is one of the most satisfying feelings a human can experience.

Is this something you might be interested in?

Let's discuss a little bit about the group. The group B individuals seem to be in a never-ending battle or struggle with life. It seems that they have to muster great effort to produce even the simplest results they want—for example, their rent, food, and basic necessities. On top of this, they seldom get any luck to help them out. They find themselves investing large quantities of energy into normal, everyday activities such as relationships, which never seem to be smooth or supportive for them. Their lives seem to be more of a burden, a heavy weight, than something to be enjoyed.

Life is meant to be enjoyable and fun; we just need to know how to use the laws of life in our favour rather than against us. Because these laws do work and can benefit us, it is easier to paddle downstream than to paddle upstream. This book is going to be all about learning how to paddle downstream and achieve more of the circumstances, things, relationships, and events that we would prefer to experience in our lives. This breeds enthusiasm, health, well-being, and love.

I was raised by a meat and potatoes style very hard-working father who doesn't tolerate laziness in himself or from others. A "no pain no gain" mentality was drummed into most of us constantly; we were told that we needed to work hard in order to make it. If this mentality were accurate, we would assume that the group A individuals would be using the "no pain no gain" mentality attitude and working harder and faster than the group B individuals.

Surprisingly, this is not the case. In fact, the group B individuals invest and expend an equal amount of energy, or sometimes even more, to achieve their unsuccessful results as the group A individuals expend to achieve their success. Hmm, seems strange, doesn't it? I would even push the limits a little further and go so far as to say that it requires less energy to be successful than it does to be unsuccessful.

Groups A and B are 100 per cent successful in creating their results. However, it is obvious that there is a clear distinction between both groups. There is a mutual thread shared by both groups in that they actually both succeeded in producing results.

What does this mean?

I will go into more detail regarding the distinctions as we move through the book. We will discover that the group A individuals use their subconscious minds much differently and more effectively than the group B individuals. This may be done consciously (knowingly) or unconsciously (unknowingly). In fact, most successful people do not realise they are using the subconscious mind more effectively than or differently to anyone else. This goes back to our childhood upbringing and the conditioning that we received during this period.

As mentioned, group B individuals may focus, apply themselves, try very hard, and invest a lot of inertia and energy in every way possible. Despite all of these efforts, ironically, they find themselves not making any progress, as though they are running on a treadmill.

The nature of using the conscious mind and willpower instead of the subconscious mind's subtler, more powerful energy elements more often than not will achieve a process that goes like this: In the beginning of a project or goal, the individual or groups begin to get excited, as it appears they are making headway and producing the results wanted. However, these initial results quickly begin to plateau. As the results begin to level off, a loss of momentum may affect the psyche, producing a further loss of power. The individuals or groups may sense the decrease in power and begin to consciously apply more effort to compensate for the decreased result. This further impedes the results they are looking for. This is the opposite of what is needed to produce the results they would prefer. Once this is noticed, it is then brought to the awareness of the conscious mind, and it becomes something we can transform.

Changing does not yield the results necessary to experience the profound shifts that we are looking for. In the realm of personal development, you'll hear the two words "change" and "transformation" used quite often. I want to make sure you understand the difference between the two. It's not that complicated, but it's sure worth clarifying.

Whenever you hear the word "change", one way you can understand it is this: it refers to changing something like your behaviour or the way you feel. It means that you alter your actions or your reactions.

Transformation, on the other hand, means something much more profound. When you transform, you expand your dimensions and your limits regarding the possibility of becoming more of yourself. I know this probably makes no sense at all. See if you can understand it easily with the aid of the following two metaphors.

Although this book appears to be about change, and in a way it is, it is more accurately not about transformation. You need to make only one small change in order for the whole to be transformed. For example, if you have a pyramid with four yellow sides and you change one sides of the pyramid to the colour red, how would you describe the change made to the pyramid?

The old way of thinking would be that the pyramid now has three yellow sides and one red side, the latter of which changed. The idea that will allow us to make changes and receive better results is this: the pyramid has now completely transformed into something new; it is now a whole new concept that it was not previous to this small change.

It is now a completely new pyramid. Thus, when we make any change within ourselves, we make a change to the whole of ourselves, and this is called a shift.

What is meant by the word "shift"? "Shift" means "to experience an expansion of awareness to another level of possibility that was not known prior". This then provides you with a choice to explore the new possibilities which supersede the previous limited view, enabling you to make better, more workable choices.

So why haven't we seen or noticed these expanded options, choices, and possibilities before? This is a good question, and the answer to this supports the reason the group A individuals are successful in attaining their desired goals and fluidity and the group B individuals are not. You see, group A is already using these new possibilities, and that's contributing to their consistent success.

So the next logical question would be, why is it that group B is not using the new choices and possibilities if they are available to be used? The information in this book is based on my own study and experience from me and my patients. Essentially, what we are doing here is beginning to form an understanding of ourselves from a new perspective. Observing and understanding our basic instincts and behavioural patterns in a new way opens us up to see more clearly. Once a basic understanding is formed, our foundation is strengthened and we can springboard into new areas of exploration within ourselves. From this we can begin to create magic in our lives. Real magic will literally start to show up in your life. I'm not referring to the card-trick and disappearing-act type of magic; I'm referring to the real beauty of real magic.

These foundational ideas are not difficult. In fact, there is a simplicity to them that is indeed so simple that they are often overlooked. These ideas will allow you to eliminate unnecessary things in your life and enable you to begin to enjoy life as the game it really is. Only now you will be helped to play the game much better if you want to. In other words, you will have more freedom to play with and to create from. You can exert more control over your life, environment, and well-being and begin to feel the power of being able to manifest in your life the things that you desire and love Another by-product of moving into alignment with yourself (your source) is that the more insight you gain into yourself, the more insight you gain overall. It is a perpetual positive spiral. We recognise through this process that we are all created from the same source, the same essence, the same energy. As this occurs, we become more sensitive and more respectful towards others as we realise we are all the same in our essence. Our relationships become smoother and easier, and we develop more understanding of others as we develop our understanding of ourselves.

This promotes our relationships to new exciting levels of possibility. As we develop this new understanding of ourselves and others, we have a tendency to subconsciously unify. As we start to operate from this new, more loving inner space where compassion becomes a natural urge of expression towards ourselves and our fellow human beings, it becomes a win-win situation. The subconscious mind's natural instinct is to unify in order to bring us together in unification and not separation. Our ego is based in the opposite—separation. And as we begin to understand through this process that our fellow humans and friends are all experiencing the same pain, frustration, dilemmas, heartaches, sadness, elation, grief, triumph, etc., we begin to recognise our similarities. This produces less judgement, and more compassion begins to flow through us, whilst at the same time selfishness begins to wane naturally, all by itself. This can and usually does open up other abilities as well.

So let's now focus on group B again to look at what influences that group's choices in achieving their results and compare that with group A, who are influenced by choosing a different method of action for their result. I discovered as a participant of the Landmark Forum (an education programme) the following statements, which I think are great examples of what I would like to say that explain this concept very clearly.

1. There are the things we know we know
2. There are the things we know we don't know
3. And there are the things we don't know we don't know.

It is the third point that I am particularly interested in discussing. As simple as this statement sounds, it is very powerful and profound, and it holds the answer to why many people are not truly happy with their lives. The Landmark Forum, who I believe adopted this term, goes further to say that in this realm of the things we don't know we don't know, we have blind spots. Blind spots are areas of our lives that we can't see for ourselves, yet they affect how we interact with our family, friends, and colleagues, the public, and the things we do on a daily basis.

When these blind spots are uncovered and cleared away, we are freed from constraints of the past, and new possibilities to create things for the future arise. In identifying and declaring the constraints from the past, your view of life, your thoughts, your feelings, and your actions naturally change in an immediate and powerful way. People are left with a new sense of freedom and clarity. The beautiful thing is that once a blind spot is recognised, it no longer has a hold or constraint upon you.

In hypnotherapy, we generally have the same intention for patients—to help them uncover their blind spots. This is the case because it is in the blind spots that illness and the seed of manifestation sprout. However, in hypnotherapy we use a different terminology: "becoming conscious of the unconscious mind" or "becoming aware of the unconscious mind".

The unconscious or subconscious mind is the largest and most powerful part of us. We can say that the conscious portion of the mind is the part of us that knows what we know and knows what we don't know. We can also say that the part of us that we don't know we don't know is the unconscious or subconscious mind.

CHAPTER 2

The Conscious and Subconscious Mind

It would be beneficial to dispel some of the myths of the subconscious mind and clarify what the subconscious mind does and what the subconscious mind's intentions are for us. Our emotions reside in the subconscious mind. Of course, we wouldn't want to be without love, caring, and all those other good emotions, but sometimes our emotions get us into trouble. The conscious mind cannot deal with emotions in any way; that is not part of its job. Any time we need emotion, the conscious mind flees like a rabbit on a greyhound racetrack, and thus we deal with such situations from the irrational, juvenile, but highly intelligent subconscious mind.

The subconscious has basically two primary intentions and functions, and they are equally important. One function is to protect us, and the second function is to guide us towards pleasurable experiences. This seems very simple, and it is. But this simplicity can be overbalanced, and the subconscious mind can veer off course. The subconscious mind will not know that it is off course and will continue to manifest what it thinks is correct data. This happens when the subconscious has been misguided or misinformed and forms a belief based on this information which may be true or false.

The subconscious mind will function in a way that it thinks it is protecting us, but in fact it is unknowingly guiding us in an undesirable direction in a destructive manner, forming a negative habit. It is unaware that it is doing this. The subconscious literally acts out at will what instructions it has been given. It thinks it's functioning normally and doing its job properly. There can be numerous reasons for this undesirable behaviour, but I will divide this into general main categories so that we can analyse it a little more.

Because the natural behaviour of the subconscious mind is to accept instructions literally, it does not question whether or not the information is good or bad, accurate or not, destructive or not, or positive or negative; it just follows the instructions exactly. The subconscious mind does not really make mistakes; it only acts on information that is given to it. It is just like a computer; a computer will give you correct information and answers based on the information and instructions that you give it. This is precisely how the subconscious mind works.

The subconscious mind needs to be programmed, just as a computer does, in order to function correctly. Our quality of life and our successes and failures are determined by the instructions and suggestions we receive in the subconscious mind. The most crucial time of our lives, when the subconscious mind is at its most impressionable stage, is during the period between the day we are born to our seventh birthday. Actually, to be more accurate, we are already being programmed whilst we are in the womb. However, for all intents and purposes we will say that it is from the first day we are born. During this period, the subconscious mind is highly suggestible and receptive, having not yet formed the critical faculties needed to judge. It thus receives and accepts all data from the environment, parents, siblings, and other external stimuli. So during this period, the foundations of our lives are laid and our belief systems are formed. This sets us on our course of life until we choose to become conscious and take control.

Your subconscious mind has total and complete power over your attitude towards you and your actions towards things. Your life is determined more by your subconscious mind than your conscious mind. Something else that is important to know and realise is that the subconscious mind never sleeps. It is always switched on. It works like a highly sophisticated twenty-four-hour surveillance system. In addition to that, our subconscious has the amazing ability to remember everything that has ever happened to us: everything we have ever seen, everything we have ever heard, everything we have ever felt, everything we have ever tasted, everything we have ever smelled. Furthermore, it can also recall any of that information if it needs to. After all, like I said earlier, your subconscious mind's primary intention is to protect you.

There was an interesting case documented in the USA where a child approximately in her teens was regressed by a hypnotherapist who was working alongside the CIA in unresolved murder cases. The hypnotherapist used hypnosis to regress the teenage girl back to the time when she was approximately three and a half years old, to an experience she had as a baby whilst asleep in her room in her house. A burglar had broken into her house, and her parents, awoken by the noise, came out to see what had happened. They were confronted by the burglar, and a scuffle broke out, leading to violent shouting and fighting. Both the mother and father were murdered by the burglar. The burglar then fled the scene and was never caught.

Twelve years later, this girl was able to recall stored information from her subconscious that had been recorded during this circumstance, and although she was sleeping in a another room at the time, she was able to recall all of the sounds that occurred, including the voice of the burglar. She was also able to recall some of the details of the conversation that occurred during the confrontation.

The information revealed during the hypnosis regression session resulted in some strong leads and helped the authorities identify some suspects. The suspects were called in and questioned, and they all provided DNA samples. The results of the DNA tests of one of the suspects matched DNA found at the crime scene, which led to the conviction of the perpetrator.

CHAPTER 3

The Critical Faculty

> ➤ **The Conscious Mind**

For you to get an understanding of how hypnosis works, it's important for you to understand how the mind works. Most of us never think about how the mind actually works; we basically take it for granted that it works and leave it at that. The mind actually consists of three distinct parts which all have different jobs and do different things, and sometimes these parts have a tough time communicating with each other.

Firstly we have the conscious mind, which this chapter will focus on. Right now, as you are reading and analysing these words and as they go into your mind and you form an understanding of what you're reading, you are using your conscious mind. Below the level of the conscious mind we have what is called the subconscious mind; we will discuss in greater depth later. There is also what is known as the unconscious portion of the mind. For most of the work done in hypnosis, however, we can essentially ignore the unconscious portion of the mind. The unconscious mind is the part that controls all of the automatic processes within us: the beating and rhythm of our heart, our blood circulation, our bodily growth, the growth of our hair and fingernails, and our digestive system. It even takes care of us while we are sleeping. It basically keeps us in balance and takes care of our health and well-being through things that happen within us automatically. Its purpose is to keep us functioning and alive and well.

However, here I would like to focus on the conscious mind in this chapter. So let's begin discussing what the conscious mind does and doesn't do. The conscious mind does four things and only four things. The first thing that the conscious mind does is analyse; it's the part of the mind that looks at a problem and figures out a way to solve it.

The second part of the conscious mind is the part that sometimes gets us into a little bit of trouble. In hypnosis it's referred to as the rational mind. This part of the mind gives us all of the reasons or excuses for the way we behave in any particular situation or circumstance. Note that yes, I did use the word "excuses". The conscious mind is set on having reasons for the things we do; it has to make sense out of what we're doing.

The third portion of our conscious mind is what we call willpower.

Finally, the fourth part of the conscious mind is what we call working memory. This is the part of the memory that we need to use daily for our everyday activities and duties: remembering how to drive to work and how to drive home again, remembering the names of people we know, remembering our telephone numbers, etc. This is the area of memory that we use and need just to get through each and every day efficiently.

This is all that the conscious mind does; it does nothing else. It's logical and analytical, and it is completely devoid of emotion and feeling.

Hypnotherapy and NLP use a commonly known term: CF. This is an abbreviation used for what is known in the field as the critical faculty or critical factor. This is a term we use in hypnosis, but most people will be more familiar with the term "conscious mind" or "analytical mind"; this is the same thing as the critical faculty.

➤ What Is the Critical Faculty?

To put it simply, the critical faculty is the part of the human mind that acts and performs as a filter. Its sole priority and function is to accept or reject incoming information based on the alignment of the information with the subconscious mind and to decide whether that information should be allowed entrance into the subconscious mind or rejected. It kind of runs a checklist system to find out whether the information is compatible with ways of thinking previously stored within the subconscious mind.

Our belief systems and values are what the CF looks for, and if the new information is compatible, it is accepted and allowed in. However, if the new information does not correspond with and match the already established beliefs and values, it rejects it and does not allow that information access to the subconscious mind.

Your critical factor plays an important role in identifying what you already feel to be true about yourself, others, and the outside world, and if this does not match and conflicts with the subconscious programming, it will place this information into a category of "false" or "untrue".

➤ Facts about the Critical Faculty

The job of the critical faculty is to stop all suggestions coming in before they enter the subconscious mind. It is euphemistically known as the "guardian of the gates", and it prevents suggestions from entering the subconscious mind. Before any suggestions are allowed past the critical faculty, a communication occurs between the critical faculty and the subconscious mind. The critical faculty asks the subconscious mind if the suggestions are allowed in. If the suggestions are congruent with the subconscious mind, they are allowed in; however, if they are not congruent with the subconscious mind, the critical faculty will block any suggestions from coming in and passing through into the subconscious mind. It is really important for the critical faculty to perform this task, because if the suggestions are allowed into the subconscious mind, a behaviour pattern will be permanently changed on the subconscious level.

The subconscious mind scans all of the memory banks to see if the incoming suggestion is congruent with the memories. If it is not, it will ask the critical faculties to reject the suggestion. However, if the suggestion is congruent with the memory banks, the suggestion is allowed into the subconscious and a change permanently takes place on the subconscious level.

Interestingly, if the subconscious rejects the suggestion, the critical faculty will then send a suggestion over to willpower and then attempt to enforce the new behaviour with willpower. So the question is, how do we get a suggestion beyond the critical factor and into the all-powerful subconscious mind? The answer is hypnosis! During hypnosis, suggestions bypass the critical faculty and enter the subconscious mind.

Here are some facts about the critical faculty; we will clear some of these up here and now. Firstly, let's focus on the benefits of the critical faculty. As I just mentioned, the critical faculty is often referred to as the guardian of the gates or the gatekeeper, and this is why: the primary function of the critical faculty is to protect you from harmful influences affecting your subconscious mind. Think about it; if you did not have a critical faculty, anyone could influence the way you think, feel, believe, and behave. You would not have the ability to choose what information you wanted to accept and what information you did not want to accept. You also would not be able to distinguish between what you think is true and what you do not think is true. You could easily end up entangled in all sorts of undesirable things.

Now that we have looked at the beneficial aspects of the critical faculty, let us shine some light on the more negative aspects. Not all of the previously stored information contained within the subconscious mind is useful. Some of the content that affects the way we think, feel, and believe can be a hindrance in moving towards our goals. It is neither helpful nor useful in helping us gain what we want. More often than not, we find it extremely difficult to change these comfortable patterns of habit. A habit is not a habit when you know you have it. It is then called a choice. You only have a habit if you don't know you have it.

➤ The Good and the Bad about the Critical Factor

Let us look at the good parts about the critical factor first. We should be thankful that we have a critical factor, because it protects us from potentially harmful influences from the outside. Consider this for a moment: if there were no CF protecting us, we would be rendered vulnerable and unprotected to outside influences. This would thus allow those influences to change the way we feel about and perceive things—even our beliefs and behaviours. We would find living this way difficult, as we would not have the ability to choose what information we wanted to accept and what information we did not want to accept. We also would find it very difficult to differentiate between what we think is true and what we do not think is true. It is good to have a critical factor playing its valuable judgemental role in protecting our privacy of mind then, is it not?

Now that we have discussed some of the positive and beneficial effects of the critical faculty, let us now discuss some of the less functional, or less desirable, parts. The fact is, not all of the previously stored information contained within the subconscious mind that affects the way we think, feel, and believe is always helpful to us, or even useful for that matter. Often we would actually like to change the way that we think, feel, believe, and behave. More often than not, we find it to be extremely difficult to do so.

The reason for this is that the CF, despite its good intentions, can be very resistant to change. Yes, we know that it has good intentions and wants to protect us and keep everything in good order and comfortable for our survival and well-being. The CF works with familiarity based on what we have already experienced in the past, such as our feelings, beliefs, thinking, and the way we respond and react to situations, circumstances, and events. It then calculates what has previously worked well for us. The critical factor will avoid disturbances so as not to let anything "rock the boat", so to speak.

This is where the CF falls short of being friendly, in a way. This can be problematic when you have decided you really want to make some changes to better your life and circumstances and you know that these changes would be of benefit and a positive decision. As I mentioned earlier, any new information or changes have to go through the filter system of the CF in order to reprogram the subconscious mind so that the changes you make will be lasting and permanent changes. These changes can only be permanent changes if they are made and accepted on the subconscious level.

So why is this so significant? This is significant because from birth to approximately seven years of age, the subconscious mind is completely open. Children in this age range absorb directly into the subconscious mind everything in their environment via the sensory perceptions (hearing, sight, taste, touch, and smell). This means that children treat everything heard by or said to them as literal or factual. Children's minds truly are like sponges. Whatever gets into their minds sticks! It becomes the truth, as there is no CF to judge or distinguish fact from fiction or error, and thus children treat the data received as accurate. They then begin to form belief patterns around the data. The more children are in contact with the data, the more the data is reinforced in the subconscious, and the stronger the belief is ingrained into the psyche.

Up to two years of age, the child learns about himself and his environment predominantly through motor and reflex actions. Thought derives from sensation, movement, and feelings sensed. The child learns that he is separate from his environment and looks to the adults, family members, siblings, authority figures, and caregivers as guides. Relationships are essential for all children. According to international child development expert Dr T. Berry Brazelton, consistent, nurturing relationships are the cornerstones of child development. Only in the context of relationships can a child survive, learn, and grow. The quality of the relationship between a child and his or her caregiver determines what the child learns about the world.

If the child is exposed to negative caregivers or environments, the child senses this, takes it on board, and begins to foster and develop these characteristics. The child may then learn to be fearful, aggressive, anxious, or passive, which may curb his curiosity.

On the contrary, a positive, nurturing environment in early childhood is likely to produce a well-adjusted, happy child. Despite genetic predispositions, the child will learn to feel safe and secure and that he or she is worth responding to.

Unbeknown to the child, despite the fact that the child may have been raised in a positive environment or a negative environment, all of this experience takes place in the subconscious mind of the child, and there is no conscious idea that this has taken place. By the time the child has reached age seven, he will have had many experiences and thus developed a set of conditioned beliefs and behaviour patterns. These beliefs are what will control the child from this point forward. In other words, the future experiences of the child will be formed and created based on the beliefs that were formed through this period. When the child matures into adolescence, he has no idea that this is so. The child begins to operate from the conscious mind, oblivious to the subconscious programming and conditioning he has bought into. No matter what direction his conscious mind wants to go in, the undertow of the powerful subconscious will always win out in the long haul. So if you have been lucky enough to have been programmed and conditioned with powerful, loving, caring relationships and caregivers, you will be programmed for success by default. On the contrary, if you were programmed with a negative, unloving environment or caregivers, you will be programmed to experience struggle, difficulty, and frustration in general. You may find that whatever you attempt to do just doesn't turn out as you expected.

You may be wondering at this stage what my point is and why I have gone through the process of explaining this.

Well, this is why: to make any transformation occur, we have to understand how and why we have got to the current place of where we are in ourselves and life. One of the best ways to understand something is to find a good analogy for it in order to see that it is like something that we already understand.

One of the things that helps us better understand how to direct the subconscious is discovering that the subconscious mind works like a storage unit, similar to a hard drive on your computer. Information is collected through our various senses and simply stored.

I have often heard it said that "the human brain is the most powerful supercomputer on the planet. The problem is we just never got the user's manual". And we were never taught in school how to use it, because our teachers never had a user's manual either. Our minds have basically been on random default. We have been letting our minds run rampant with little to no true direction and, more to the point, limited knowledge of how to correct any of the issues created by this lack of understanding.

If we look at the subconscious mind as simply a tool and move away from the stigma of being an entity with good or bad intentions, we can begin to understand how to use it to our benefit.

Another similarity to the computer is that when the information is stored in your subconscious mind, it is indexed so that when your conscious mind needs specific information, there is a pathway to retrieve it.

Another attribute worth knowing is that the subconscious mind does not place any value judgement on the information it is given. It doesn't look at the information and go, "Okay . . . this is good, this is bad, this is right, and this is wrong." Your subconscious mind simply stores it. It also does not determine how it is stored. Just like a computer, it takes the information given to it, just as it is given. And just like a computer, if you make an error in the data you are giving it, your unconscious will simply accept the error as what you intended for it to be given.

Now we understand that the subconscious mind is simply storing information, and that it never switches off. This means that every experience we have ever had has been collected and stored in the subconscious mind. These experiences are available as references and resources for us as we progress in our lives. And here is where the lack of a user's manual begins to become a problem.

Since we have not been taught how to correctly tap into those resources, we usually do the best we can based on the resources we have. We have heard that we get what we focus on, but we have not truly been taught how to direct our focus in ways that allow us to get what we truly desire. In fact, here is a rule that is surprising but true: you get what you focus on, and what you focus on grows.

But if you focus on something you don't want, you actually get want you don't want. This is a very common error that creates a lot of frustration.

For example, when we are focused on what we don't want, that is all we see, and our ideas and decisions are based on what we don't want. When we know what we want, we give ourselves the ability to imagine new possibilities and generate ideas on how to be and what to do or say in each moment to make it a reality.

The subconscious mind works with images, pictures, and emotions to create your reality. So when you focus on something that you don't want, you are focusing on a picture in your mind that you do not want. And remember, because the subconscious mind does not judge information but accepts it as it is, it will begin to manifest the negative image.

For example, if I say to you, "Don't think of a pink cat," what happens? Yes, you think of a pink cat. You have to hold it in your mind not to think of it.

By learning how to direct the conscious mind, we can begin to gain access to the true strengths that are available to us in our subconscious libraries. So what specifically do I mean when I refer to the way in which we direct the conscious mind? We ultimately have the capacity to choose what we focus on. It is said that we take in over 10 million bytes of information per second. And as a matter of survival and the ability to function, the conscious mind, subconscious mind, and supra-conscious mind all have specific information designated to them. We have also been given the ability to filter the information we take in, bringing the specific information we are focusing on into our dominant areas of focus, while we process the rest of the information without giving it much attention.

So where we are and what we are doing in life is influenced and controlled by the beliefs that we hold in our subconscious minds.

We have established that man is very similar to a computer. In fact, we could say more accurately that the computer is made in the image of man. Man has a body, and so does a computer. Man has a brain, and so does a computer. (The computer's brain is the hard drive.) A computer has a program, and so does a man. (The man's program is the subconscious mind.)

The good news is that just as a computer can easily be updated and reprogrammed to perform better and deliver new results, we can also perform better by changing the default program within the subconscious mind.

CHAPTER 4

How Our Memory Contributes

The recall of memory and its efficiency, capabilities, and capacity for memorisation are directly related to and closely associated with the subconscious mind. Therefore, I would like to reveal some very interesting behaviours relating to our memories and recall. These behaviours are so habitual to us that we are unaware of their presence. These very interesting behaviours which I have come across in my hypnotherapy work can be duplicated in tests and are predictable in behaviour and outcome. However, there's no need to try to prove this theory, because you have probably had one of these experiences before, and maybe more than one time. You will more than likely know exactly what I'm talking about as I explain this to you.

Have you ever had an experience where you have been preparing for an examination or a test and this has happened: Just prior to entering the examination room, you are feeling quite confident. You studied well and you know all of your material. However, as you enter the examination room, you feel the change in atmosphere and maybe feel a little tension in the air from other students or people in the room. Then, as you sit down to begin the examination, all of a sudden your mind goes completely blank. The more you try to recall information, the more frustrating it becomes, and you just cannot recall the information that you need for the exam.

Or you may have had a slightly different experience. Perhaps you have been studying and learning a new skill, such as a dance routine or a martial arts kata, and you are ready to take your examination. It may be an exam or test for which you have to perform certain movements. For some unknown reason, your mind goes blank whilst you're performing and you completely forgot a portion or all of the routine, even though you are sure you knew it all flawlessly and had practised it many times perfectly before. You may have even practised it for years, to the point of complete mastery.

Although this may have seemed to be an anomaly at the time, there is a very simple and logical explanation as to why this happens. And this will make perfect sense to you once explained.

When people prepare for their studies, they generally choose a location or environment that is conducive to studying. A quiet room, a relaxed atmosphere, and maybe some familiar objects and personal items in the room make them feel relaxed and comfortable. Some people enjoy having their favourite music playing, and maybe have some coffee or snacks just in a reach, et cetera.

There is a common thread that begins to reveal itself as I describe more of the attributes related to the study scene. Looking at this closely, you can notice that relaxation is the common thread. We draw upon our natural instincts by using our senses to create as peaceful or relaxed an environment as possible. The clever subconscious mind knows that we need to relax and calm our conscious mind for it to function more efficiently, so we do whatever it takes for us to relax and make it as enjoyable as possible to study. We may not even give this a second thought; we could do it without even noticing this behaviour.

Being in this particular location and this state of relaxation forms what we term in hypnosis an "anchor". All of the senses of the body-touch, sight, smell, taste, and hearing—are involved in this activity of study.

The subconscious mind takes all this information and stores it in a certain part of the mind. It also attaches all the information that is being studied at the same time, storing that information in that same compartment. It links the data and the information that is being studied and received through the senses with the information of the senses and then compartmentalises all of this information under one heading and anchors it all together in that location as one chunk of information.

When we enter the examination room or the location where we will be tested on this information, an interesting thing occurs. Because the environment is different to the environment where the study took place while the student was in a state of relaxation, when the student searches for the information in the mind, he is not able to access the compartment where all the information from the studying has been stored. He is not able to access that information because the information is stored in a compartment of the mind which is relaxed. When the individual sits for the examination, his state changes from a relaxed state to a different state. He may have developed some anxiety or tension. In this different state of mind, there is no access to the information required for the examination, because it is in that relaxed compartment of the mind. And thus, the student sitting for the examination draws a blank. This then elevates the state into a more anxious state because of the frustration of not being able to access the information and the pressure of the time constraint of the exam. This then pushes the information even further out of reach, rendering the individual mindless, so to speak.

This is a very easy situation to solve, and I have had tremendous results with my clients in my hypnosis sessions with these anchors. Anchors are one of my favourite techniques to use because they are so efficient and can be so powerful, and yet they are easy to use.

Remember, I mentioned that the natural and instinctive process of the subconscious mind it is to absorb all of the information held in focus via the senses, link it to the information from the state of mind the individual is in at the time, and then anchor it. The key is then to be able use the anchor to your advantage whenever you want to.

CHAPTER 5

Anchors and States

➢ **What Are Anchors?**

Just to reiterate, an anchor is an association to any life experience or memory. Anchors are composed using all of our senses. When applying an anchor, the greater number of senses used, the stronger it will be. Anchors can be installed by using the spoken word. In fact, without even realising it, we are being manipulated on a day-to-day basis by our own word anchors. Have you ever felt sick or bad when someone has said someone else's name? Or you may have felt really good and felt a pleasant emotion. Or you may have even experienced both of these feelings. These are examples of anchors in effect.

A hypnotic anchor is a created psychological mechanism representing that link we are describing. Such an anchor can be installed intentionally or covertly. The practitioner observes emotions or states of minds and then sets the trigger—a special action or series of actions that can be used later to invoke the same state or response. The effect of this is that you can learn to influence feelings, states of consciousness, or habits.

When a person feels a negative emotion when he hears the utterance of someone's name (an anchor), all of that negative emotion that was previously linked to that person is stimulated. And of course it works for positive feelings as well. Here is another example: If I mention the word "grandma", what happens in your mind? Your subconscious mind kicks in, and you may all of a sudden see the image of your grandma in her warm, clean kitchen across the other side of the country, dressed in her white-and-blue pinstriped cooking overalls, baking your favourite cookies as she always does on Sunday afternoons. You begin to catch that sweet sent, the aroma of those delicious cookies filling the warm kitchen. This then sends a warm, comfortable signal to your body—particularly your stomach area—and you begin to feel a nice sensation occurring there. And before you even realise it, your mouth is salivating.

The procedure for installing an anchor for therapeutic or change work is quite simple. Here is an example of one method in a therapeutic hypnotherapist-to-client context.

The client is asked to visualise his favourite place of relaxation—a place where everything is comfortable and he feels perfectly safe (the keyword being "relaxation"). The hypnotherapist then elicits the state of relaxation and deepens the feeling, creating a state of change in the client. Once the desired state of change is reached (which the hypnotherapist will know), the hypnotherapist will install the anchor trigger at the peak of the required state.

Once the anchor has been installed, the process is complete. The client can either remain in the changed state to enjoy it or resume a waking conscious state. The next step is to draw the client's attention to a completely different topic or situation to distract the client, to focus him on a completely different feeling and state—one closer to a normal conscious state. This can be done as easily as asking him a simple question, such as "What is your phone number backwards?"

The next step is to test the anchor and notice the immediate state change in the client. (The client will also experience the state change.)

CHAPTER 6

Hypnosis

Although this is not a book entirely dedicated to hypnosis, I do think it would be beneficial to have a chapter on hypnosis included in the book so as to provide a basic understanding of hypnosis based on the premise that we use hypnosis every day knowingly or unknowingly without much awareness of doing so. It is such a natural part of our behaviour that, more often than not, we don't even realise we use it. We are in hypnosis more often than you might believe.

To gain a better understanding of how hypnosis works, it will be helpful for you to understand how your mind works.

We have three very separate and very distinct minds. They do different and separate things, and because of this, they sometimes have difficulty relating to and communicating with each other.

The conscious mind is the first portion; this is where you are right now. Below that level of awareness is the subconscious mind. And then an even deeper part of us—in fact the deepest part of us—is the unconscious mind.

For the purposes of basic hypnosis, we are not going to discuss the unconscious mind in much detail, but it's the part of us that controls the automatic body functions. It controls the strength or weakness of the immune system, and it controls the automatic body functions, such as the heartbeat, the blinking of the eyes, and other things like this.

The conscious mind is where we spend most of our time. I want you to understand that it basically does only four things and no more. The first thing it does is analyse. What is that? Well, that is the act of looking at problems and figuring out ways to solve them. It is also the part of us that makes the hundreds of decisions we have to make to get through an average day—decisions we think are automatic but, in fact, are not. This includes decisions like, "Should I open the door?" "Should I turn the water on?" and "Should I wear these shoes?" We might think those are automatic functions, but we must make a decision as to whether or not we want to do these things.

The second part of the conscious mind is a part that can sometimes get us into a little difficulty and trouble. It's known as the rational portion of the conscious mind. This portion of the mind must supply us with a reason to justify why we behave in any particular way. You see, if we don't have a reason for behaving in a certain way and for doing the things that we do, it creates anxiety, nervousness, and frustration in the mind, and if this goes on long enough, it can create imbalances in our systems. This can lead to illness if it is not detected in time and corrected.

The only problem with the reasons the rational mind gives us as to why we behave in any particular fashion is that they are never original. For example, a smoker may say smoking relaxes him because it calms him and gives him time to pause and gather his thoughts. An overweight person may say he is overweight because he eats when bored, because he eats when nervous, or because he digests slowly. The problem with such reasons is that they are never the original problem. Before the smoker developed his habit, he heard other people that smoked say, "I smoke because it makes me feel calm and relaxed." Or he heard an overweight person say, "I'm overweight because I eat when I'm nervous."

Hypnotherapists can see through these transparent reasons, and we understand and know why people are smokers, are overweight, etc. We generally get all the security we need when we grow up in a nice family. But usually when we arrive at the age of twelve or thirteen, our parents don't seem as smart as they used to, so we shut off our ability to gain security from those individuals and instead seek security by becoming part of a group of kids at school. If we feel that we don't belong to this particular group or tribe, it is because of the subconscious mind. The subconscious is a very interesting part of us; it must protect us against danger, and not getting the necessary security we need is a definite danger to us.

Frequently the subconscious mind will substitute one form of security in place of another. The inner dialogue of the mind then becomes something like, "Smokers are accepted and secure." When that happens, the next time someone offers you a cigarette and you take it, you immediately feel that you are part of a group and your security level goes up. It really has nothing to do with being calm or relaxed on the core level.

So understand that the reason the rational mind gives us for why we behave in a particular fashion is never original and nearly always incorrect. You don't start smoking because it makes you feel calm; you start because you need security!

The third part of the conscious mind is commonly known as willpower. Yes, we have all heard of willpower, haven't we. It goes something like this: You say to yourself, "I'm going to give up smoking these awful cigarettes, and I'm giving them up forever." Well, how long does that last before you begin smoking again? How many of you have tried dieting using not just one diet method but perhaps several? Again, how long do the results last? They last just until the willpower weakens, and then the old habit comes back again. But this time, it also establishes a negative belief system of failure in the mind, and this brings an emotional and mental feeling of defeat into the subconscious. This then makes any further efforts to quit smoking or make a successful diet programme work even more difficult. Each time there is a failure with the use of willpower, there is also a stored recording of the failure on the subconscious level as well.

The fourth and last part of the conscious mind is what is known as the conscious working memory. That's the memory we need and use for simple everyday tasks, such as getting to work, recalling the names of people we know, and remembering our phone numbers. It is the memory we need just to get through an average day.

This is all that the conscious mind does. It does nothing else. Our conscious mind is very logical and very analytical and frequently wrong. Where the *real* you, me, and everyone else lives is in the level below the conscious mind, called the subconscious mind.

➢ What Is Hypnosis?

The subconscious mind is like a video recorder. It records all of our life experiences via our five senses. Even whilst we sleep, the subconscious continues to record sounds and other stimuli via our senses. The subconscious mind is also influenced and picks up on other people's ideas and belief systems. It may accept them as being true, as the subconscious mind has no ability to judge or rationalise between right and wrong or true and false. Thus, some of these beliefs may be, and usually are, self-limiting or self-sabotaging beliefs. This set of beliefs is developed most predominately during early childhood. These belief systems may or may not be true for us; however, they set the tone and foundation for the rest of our lives—unless we change them.

The reason hypnotherapy works so well is that it not only deals with the current issues, belief systems, and behaviours effectively and quickly, but it also deals with these belief systems and influences—and any emotion and trauma associated with them—from an early age. This enables the hypnotherapist to reach in and clear out the root cause, which commonly results in emotional and mental relief, and also physical healing of any symptoms that were related to the issue.

Hypnosis is a completely natural but altered state of mind that is similar to sleep, which is an altered state of mind. But when you are in hypnosis, you are not asleep at all. Hypnosis alters your state of consciousness in such a way that the analytical left-hand side of the brain is distracted or bypassed, while the more creative right-hand side is made more alert. The conscious mind is diverted or distracted, whilst the subconscious mind is woken up. Since the subconscious mind is much more powerful and determines your habits, emotions, feelings, unconscious behaviours, and attitudes, it is here in the subconscious mind that we hypnotherapists do positive change work.

With a subject in the relaxed state of hypnosis, I bypass the subject's conscious mind to gain a direct connection with the subconscious mind. The next step of the process is to implement the new suggestions of change to create a new path or direction neurolinguistically (via the neural pathway in the brain). The positive suggestions of change begin to create new feelings, emotions, and directions within you as the new neural pathways are created, leaving the old patterns to dissolve naturally, unleashing you to be free of those old burdens. One of the beautiful things about hypnosis change work is that the new positive changes require no willpower or strain on your behalf; the new change work becomes aligned within you as a natural part of you. It becomes your second nature once the suggestions have been accepted on the subconscious level.

The reason hypnotherapy works so well is that it deals with not only the learned behaviour but also any emotion and trauma associated with it, clearing out the root cause and empowering you to integrate a healthier mindset for the future.

➢ What Can Hypnosis Do for Me?

During a self-hypnosis trance, your brain generates different levels of brainwave activity. One of these levels is called alpha waves. This state is created when your body becomes relaxed. A self-hypnosis trance state includes heightened levels of focus and awareness. The difference between ordinary focus and self-hypnosis trance is your focus. You will lose focus on the things that are happening around you and concentrate all your focus on one thing.

Right now, in this conscious state, whilst you are concentrating on reading these words, you are fully focused on what you are reading, and you have entered a very light state of self-hypnosis; it's a mild trance state. This is a natural and very useful ability. Did you ever learn to drive a car or motorbike? Think back to when you first learned this; there were many things to remember, and it was awkward and difficult, right? It was necessary to focus and concentrate on the physical mechanics of driving the automobile: watching all around you and in the mirrors for other drivers, accelerating smoothly and depressing the clutch in time with the gear change, steering straight (sometimes with only one arm), watching traffic signals and signposts, etc. It was necessary to broaden your focus and peripheral vision to include many different things. We are certainly lucky we don't have to do this with every task we perform throughout the day; this could become rather exhausting, to say the least.

Fortunately we have the ability to focus and concentrate on one or two subjects and place all of our attention on that particular point. This enables us to allow everything else that is going on around us to continue as it is. You may have observed a secretary in action in an office; she can answer the phones whilst typing something else on the computer keyboard, stacking papers and moving them around the desk, and conversing with a colleague in right next to her, and yet none of these things seems to affect her efficiency in getting her job done well.

If self-hypnosis were not possible, then the ability to multitask would not exist. We would constantly be distracted by things going on all around us. Being "in the zone", or self-hypnosis, assists us to deepen a light trance state into a deeper trance state so that we can focus more clearly and sharper on a chosen subject.

An additional benefit of being in this light trance state or "in the zone" is that it makes us more susceptible and open to accepting suggestion because we are in an alpha brainwave mode.

Therefore we begin to utilise the self-hypnosis state to

- absorb, learn, and retain data more easily,
- learn and redirect new habits,
- improve memory recall,
- increase self-confidence,
- improve sporting abilities,

- eradicate negative behaviours,
- increase healing speed,
- reverse the ageing process,
- increase positive manifestations,
- improve relationships with ourselves and others,
- improve financial income,
- change destructive habits,
- improve our immune systems,
- create and sculpt the body we like,
- improve sleeping,
- reduce stress and anxiety,
- increase energy levels,

and much more.

CHAPTER 7

Thought vs. Thinking

Commonly, we humans stop and apply the process of thinking only when we are confronted with a difficult situation, a problem, or a situation outside the comfort zone of our normal regular behaviour and instinctive or habitual circumstance.

Thinking is characteristically the tool of choice or method that we resort to for seeking solutions, as opposed to the haphazard, unconscious, hit-or-miss, instinctual method common in the rest of the animal world. It is this power of dealing with a particular situation by contemplation and reflection that distinguishes the human being from the animal; we can be conscious of our consciousness.

The kind of thinking then that is being considered here is controlled, constructive thinking directed towards the solution of a problem. The problem may be practical or theoretical. It may involve repairing a piece of furniture or an engine, finding the answer to a problem in a crossword puzzle, solving a Rubik's cube, balancing a mathematics equation, or constructing a poem or song; the list is endless. The ability to think clearly and rationally is important no matter what we choose to use it for.

If you work in education, research, finance, management, or the legal profession, then clear thinking is obviously important. Being able to think well and solve problems systematically is an asset for any career. Thoughts, properly thought through in a conscious way, are a very powerful tool. Problems arise when thinking gets out of hand and the thinking begins to manage the thinker rather than the thinker being in control and managing the thoughts and thinking.

For example, have you ever heard a person say that he thinks too much or finds it difficult to stop thinking? You may have even said it yourself or to someone else in an innocuous manner. More than likely, many of us have experienced that uncomfortable feeling of having many thoughts bombarding and criss-crossing through our minds in all ways, shapes, and sizes, coming in from all directions. It leaves us feeling like we just want to escape from it. But how do you escape from something that is part of you, inside of you? If you have experienced this, you know well that it is difficult to escape. There seems to be no hiding from these thoughts; wherever you go, the thoughts follow too.

This whirlwind of thoughts flowing in from all angles can be an overwhelming feeling. It appears there is no escape from these tenacious little critters called thoughts because it's an internal experience connected so intimately with us. If we were able to manage and control our thinking in a more comfortable manner, the immediate benefits would be evident. Improved focus and concentration would also be an immediate beneficial by-product. With improved focus and concentration alone, we can create dramatic improvements in our quality of life. Also, productivity would increase favourably, and many other positive benefits would be assured. It is common for us to find ourselves being entangled in this chaos of thoughts and processes, which leaves us with a feeling of being out of touch with ourselves. Our minds seem to be more in control of us and using us, rather than us using and controlling our minds, which is the way it was meant to be.

Most of us are under the delusion that we think we use our minds; however, most of the time our minds are using us and we don't even know it. It is rare to find a person that is conscious of this, and rarer still to find a person who will admit to it. I am not pointing the finger or judging; there is no right or wrong. The intention is to point out and distinguish that which works best for us and what doesn't work to benefit us. If you are one of these people who falls into this category of being used by your mind, there is no need to feel bad. You may feel better knowing that the status quo has accepted this way of functioning as normal. However, relief is nigh; it is clear that the balance of the scales is beginning to tilt towards a new direction of great change.

This constant barrage of thoughts and energy is also commonly known as "mind chatter". It can also be called the "inner voice" or "inner dialogue" (not to be confused with the highly beneficial intuitive inner voice, which is an entirely different voice and feeling altogether).

This phenomenon not only affects our mental abilities, but it also has a direct affect on how our bodies move and feel. So what effect would a cluttered and congested mind have on the body? It would, of course, produce a sluggish, congested body. The mind becomes slow and sluggish because it has no space to work; there are not even any spaces between the thoughts. And when this becomes chronic it becomes one of the major causes of stress, headaches, migraines, digestive disorders, and many other imbalances and diseases. There is a lack of ease in mind, and therefore there is a lack of ease in the body—hence "disease". As the body becomes more difficult to manoeuvre, we have to find more energy to push the body to function normally in everyday tasks. This is one of the reasons that many people find themselves feeling tired even though they seem to be getting enough sleep and eating a fairly well-balanced diet.

This is not the whole picture yet, but believe it or not, this process is a continuous cycle, as we repeat the same thoughts over and over. In fact, National Science Foundation statistics show that out of 100 per cent of our thinking process, 90 per cent is *negative* thinking and approximately 90 per cent is repetitive. Now, if you understand that our thinking creates our reality, and if you do the maths, it is not a sunny outlook, to say the least. After discovering this statistic, my first question was, how are we surviving with so few positive thoughts in our lives?

After digging around for some more information about this, I came across some interesting related information. The potency and power of a single positive thought is tremendously more powerful than a negative thought. And this is where things begin to take a turn for the best, so to speak. Just as it seemed this was all going to be doom and gloom, there is good news to share. The good news is that we can learn how to manage and control our thoughts so that they benefit us.

CHAPTER 8

The Witness State

"The witness state" is the term used for observing or witnessing the play of the mind or the activity of the mind. The witness is the thoughtless observer within us, or a state of being in consciousness that is purely witnessing the chattering of the mind without interfering, judging, or contemplating. Being in a state of complete acceptance without personal predispositions is highly beneficial. This may sound very spiritual or out of reach, as though you may need to embark upon a spiritual journey to learn this. On the contrary, it is very simple to do, and you can practise this with yourself with great proficiency. By simply learning to step back from the mind chatter you can begin to feel relief and ease in your mind, heart, and body as it begins to settle and relaxes into a normal, balanced state.

Picture this for a moment: the mind is in constant flux and has built up momentum like a heavy rolling wheel. Similarly, it is like asking a fish what the water is like. This is impossible for the fish to answer, as it has always known only the water and therefore has no reference point for comparison. So this momentum, as we have said, is seldom recognised or noticed by us. The idea, then, is that when you become a witness or observer to the thoughts and momentum of thoughts or processes, you create a distance, or buffer zone, outside of this whirlwind of mind activity.

By entering this witness state, you stop adding further energy and fuel to the momentum of the thought streams. The thoughts begin to slow down, and the restlessness of the mind gradually decreases until a gap can form in between the thought streams. This gap is very important. Within this gap, tranquillity and will are finally found. When these gaps appear, a feeling of profound peace and clarity is experienced. And there is actually a name for this next stage; it is called the state of thoughtless awareness.

As mentioned earlier regarding the sluggish mind causing the body to be sluggish as well, one of the benefits and side effects that I experienced as I practised the witness state was the freeing up of my body along with my mind. I felt more energy beginning to flow through my body. This was a welcome relief, as previous to this I was one of those individuals that wrestled with a sluggish body and felt tired for no apparent reason. Another negative side effect of an overload of thinking is stress and weakening of the immune or nervous systems. This makes a person more susceptible to common colds, flu, and allergies.

CHAPTER 9

Self-Talk?

What is inner self talk? We awaken in the mornings and go about our daily duties and tasks in our lives, and as we do, we have a constant stream of thoughts going through our minds, internally chatting about this and that, discussing, negotiating, surveying, and calculating all of the situations, circumstances, and events going on around us. In fact, the situations that the self-talk pertains to may not even be right in front of us; the situations could pertain to planning for the future or even thinking about the past. This is what is known in the hypnotherapy, psychology, and spiritual areas as unconscious and conscious self-talk. Most people are usually unaware that they are in this mode of self-talk, because it can run rather deep from the conscious mind all the way down to the unconscious. So it's not unusual for people to not even realise they are doing it. The self-talk is best described as a constant internal dialogue or internal voice inside ourselves or inside our minds that measures and gauges how we receive information from our surroundings and how we then perceive this through our own unique filtering systems. This inner voice is commonly referred to and known as self-talk, and as I said, it includes our conscious thoughts as well as our unconscious and subconscious thoughts.

Because of this constant, relentless stream of untamed thoughts flowingly in, there is data and information consistently washing around inside the mind. This can sometimes become a bit like a leaky tap that has been left running unknowingly. The constant mind chatter allows a lot of our vital energy and power to leak out. This can lead to our health being knocked out of balance, weakening the immune system, which can then result in stress, allowing other illnesses the opportunity to enter. It is important to maintain a healthy and balanced immune system so that we can remain healthy. The normally functioning healthy immune system is very strong and resilient; it protects us against all sorts of diseases viruses and other things in the environment that could attack us. However, when the immune system is healthy, balanced, and running smoothly, it does a fantastic job.

Since I have not exactly been praising the self-talk phenomenon in this chapter so far, it does appear to be a negative or bad thing. Although some of our self-talk seems to be bad, it does have some useful and good qualities. So, before moving ahead, let's discuss some of these more positive aspects.

We require certain self-talk, such as, "Oh, I must remember to fill up the gas tank this afternoon" or "I must remember to set my alarm clock for 5.00 a.m. tomorrow." But as we become more aware of our self-talk, we can begin to see that a lot of the self-talk is nothing but junk—especially when the self-talk has a negative flavour and is detrimental to our positive progress. Insecure or self-defeating self-talk is quite a problem with a lot of people. Some of our self-talk can be limiting and negative, and this does not really help. Different personalities, through the different conditioning processing filters, are endowed with their own unique ways of perceiving and processing environmental data.

Here are a few examples of how people can perceive things using their processing filters through their conditioning:

1. **The all-or-nothing point of perception**

   (This was one of my own negative self-talks that I used to experience a lot. I cleaned this up, thankfully, and no longer suffer from this.)

   This is what people do when they are using an all-or-nothing point of perception. They put situations into categories of black and white; there is no margin for error. If they were to perform some sort of skill and it fell short of their expectation or of perfection, they would see themselves as a complete failure.

The balancing self-talk response would be as follows:

You are aware and recognise that you gave it your best shot and learned something along the way. You can be compassionate with yourself and go easy on yourself; this changes the context of the situation, and thus the stress level of the body is reduced.

2. Critical perceptions and interpretations

This is when you concentrate or focus on a detail with a distorted perception and begin to interpret the information as negative. The object of the focus is seen inaccurately and distorted, and thus what is being observed is misinterpreted through the senses.

Correcting and reprogramming the perception:

Bring your attention to the detail that is the most attractive so that you can appreciate it; this will change the quality of the energy.

3. Rejecting, dismissing, or disqualifying yourself

(This is very common, and I had to work on this particular issue myself as well.) This refers to rejecting positive experiences, such as a friend or spouse remarking that you look great today or giving you any type of compliment or gesture of generosity. Rejecting these types of situations is created by a lack of self-esteem or a feeling of guilt. Blowing off the compliment and rejecting it seems to balance your feeling of negativity and guilt. Underlying this is a belief that you do not deserve to be complimented. This then helps you to feel a false sense of control. It sometimes can actually feel comfortable for you to do this, because it gives you a feeling that you are in control because you get the last word and make the final decision.

Correcting the response:

Keep your awareness in the moment, in present time, and as you experience these compliments flowing towards you, focus on how the energy feels as you receive it. Allow yourself to feel the positive energy, and be aware of how that feels at the time.

4. **Reacting and responding: jumping to conclusions**

This is when an individual has a habit of forming impulsive decisions, judgements, and biased opinions or interpretations with few facts to support the situation or circumstance. Here are some examples:

a. **Thinking that you can read another person's mind:**

You have decided or concluded that someone is responding negatively to your ideas or you personally, though in reality you don't have any idea if you are correct or not. This leaves you in a state of confusion and can sometimes even produce a superiority or inferiority complex to try to balance out the situation in your favour so that you feel better about yourself and the situation.

b. **Predicting the future:**

You expect that things will take a turn for the worse, and you expect that your prediction is inevitable.

The reprogrammed response:

You take on a positive disposition and decide in your mind that things are going to go well for you, that situations and circumstances will favour you and give you the advantage. If you do notice some things that seem not to be going your way, take a closer look and determine whether the situation is actually helping you to see another way of doing something, which in the long term maybe will yield a much better outcome.

5. Using "you should" statements

Shoulds and shouldn'ts, as well as the statement "I will try", should be completely eliminated from your vocabulary. If you were to do so for one month, you would see quite an amazing difference in your manifestations within a short time. Using shoulds and shouldn'ts indicates that you are already guilty before you have even attempted the action in mind; it's almost as if you are punishing yourself before you have even begun to do anything. (E.g. "I should not think about eating that dessert. I shouldn't be thinking about nice things.") The underlying force and emotional content is guilty feelings. Frustration and resentment are usually generally felt when you direct shoulds and shouldn'ts towards others. To add insult to injury, when we do use shoulds and shouldn'ts to motivate or control other people, those people generally don't listen to them and ignore them and go on doing their own thing.

The reprogrammed response:

Think of a better option that will achieve a more positive result for you in other ways, such as recalling positive events with good feelings related to the situation at hand. (E.g. "Eating dessert now and again is fine; everything is good in balance." This will result in a positive feeling that the body will respond to.)

6. Personalising

You see yourself as the cause of some unhealthy external event that you were not responsible for. (E.g. "We were late to the dinner party and caused the hostess to overcook the meal. If I had only pushed my husband to leave on time, this wouldn't have happened.")

The reprogrammed response:

> You don't take on the blame that belongs to other people. (E.g. "My husband wouldn't stop watching the football game on TV, and this made us late to the party.")

As mentioned earlier, these patterns of negative or positive self-talk often start in childhood. Usually the self-talk habit is one that's influenced our thinking for years and can affect us in many ways. However, any time can be a good time to change it. Here are some ways you can stop yourself from using negative self-talk and help place your mind in a better state for creating greater possibilities in your life.

The more you catch yourself in negative self-talk and pause to analyse why you are thinking or feeling that way, the more you can redirect yourself to positive self-talk change. Rather than criticising yourself for doing the wrong thing or making a blunder, you can begin to give yourself some room and space to make mistakes whilst being attentive to and recognising the self-talk that goes with doing so.

The amount of negative feelings and negative talk may seem overwhelming at first, but as you practise this more, it will gradually decrease. It may not cease completely, but if you use each opportunity to analyse why things went wrong, notice the negative self-talk and focus on positive opposites, as in the examples above. You will turn these opportunities into tools for improvement. Then these inner changes will begin to reflect into the outer world of daily life. Once you recognise this, it will be a major boost of encouragement to your self-esteem. Knowing that the changes you have been making inside by being aware of your self-talk are now being rewarded by more pleasing changes in everyday life is a great achievement.

Our words are literally seen and accepted as suggestions and even commands to the subconscious mind, and the subconscious mind thrives and learns by repetition. You know that people easily develop habits of using certain words and phrases over and over again. Well, imagine that we don't hear the self-talk that takes place in our internal dialogue. Words develop habits, which are a powerful way to program the mind in a conscious way. In this way you can custom design and reprogram the subconscious to suit your desires. I have found using subliminal MP3s to be a great way to do this as well.

Although the subconscious mind is far superior in intelligence and far greater in power than the conscious mind, it is in a way under the control and direction of the conscious mind; it is the conscious mind that must initiate change. This may be likened to a captain of a ship. The ship has all of the power, but the captain presides over a large crew who work the ship. The workforce has greater power but relies on the wise control and direction from the captain. It is thus advisable to become conscious and weed out all of those negative or limiting word habits. You must learn to say what you intend—or rather learn to intend consciously and speak words aligned to that—in order to have this level of manifestation work in your favour. As we discovered in the introductory chapters, the subconscious mind will take what you say literally if you repeat it enough. Several word habits to be reprogrammed are discussed below.

Following are some of the most commonly used words we use that are detrimental to us.

1. I'll try

What does it mean to try to do something? According to Merriam-Webster, it can mean "to make an attempt at" and it is often used with an infinitive (e.g. "try to fix the car"). Can you try to cook the dinner, or is it better stated that you can cook the dinner or not cook the dinner? Can you try to lift the knife and fork? Can you try to lift anything? "Try" is a strange word, really. How can you try to do something? For example, if you try to run, you will either run or not run. Maybe you can *try* to figure it out.

Try is the ultimate catch-all qualifier for anyone looking to commit absolutely nothing to a particular effort. It's not even particularly sneaky any more. We know what it means. Saying "I'll try" is a very weak commitment that implies the escape clause "I may not succeed." So when we say we'll try, the subtext is that we may well fail. Whenever you catch yourself saying "I'll try", stop and decide what your real intention is. Then commit either one way or another; the key is to be honest with yourself. When you try, your energy is connected, but it's not creating a clear forward motion, which ends up acting as an energy drain.

2. I Can't

Saying the words "I can't" sends a signal to the subconscious mind to go scouting in search of supporting evidence. The subconscious has an amazing ability to manifest and supply you with all the support and reasons you can't, to back up your intention. This then creates a self-fulfilling prophecy. The more you use "I can't", the more you will perceive and experience limitation. When you say "I can't", stop and pause for a moment and realise what you are saying. It might be a moment when you are feeling self-doubt, feeling incompetent, or maybe even thinking of past failed attempts. Whatever the situation, start to learn to practise being aware of your internal dialogue. It will be of great benefit to you and can yield amazing results. At the least, ask yourself if this is something you would like to be able to do or achieve.

3. Should or Have to

The next words to become aware of and avoid using as much as possible are "I should" and "I have to." Speaking these words automatically sends a direct, clear message to the subconscious that you are not in control of the situation at hand and that it is almost as if an outside influence or authority has power over you. A heaviness or inner resistance may be felt e or, at the very least, a sense of having to "shape up". In both cases, we set up an unconscious rebellion within. Furthermore, it is a denial of one's own inner source and own inner ability to handle the situation. This gives us the feeling that we need some external source to tell us how and what to do. Of course this is disempowering, as we reject the opportunity of being able to exercise the power of choice from our own inner source and power. Start to learn to practise awareness of your internal dialogue saying "I should", or "I have to." It will be of great benefit to you, and it can yield amazing results.

4. I am—Negatives

"Therefore I am" is a very famous quotation, and rightly so, as the I ams are very powerful commands we can speak. Every time we say these words, the subconscious mind comes to attention and begins to listen intently. Whether these words are used positively or negatively, they are powerful and command a certain listening and respect from the subconscious. When you say "I am" with a negative statement, that negative reality is immediately reinforced. There is always a verbal implication when we voice negative. "I am really tired today", "Oh, I'm so stupid", "I'm really angry": all these statements are condescending to self-approval and are declarations that little or nothing should be expected from us.

For example, "Oh, I'm so stupid" is a plea for others to not judge our stupidity and to make an assessment already based on the stupidity; in this way we have judged ourselves ahead of time. It may also be a clever way of suggesting to another person present not to expect a good job from us. What people are not aware of when doing this to themselves is that they send an unconscious suggestion to others to bolster and support their negative, limited attitude; bringing more attention to it only strengthens this negative quality.

As another example, "I am really tired today" is a warning to others to expect us to perform at a lower level of performance than usual. The verbal implication may be "I am tired; therefore, I won't perform well" or "I am tired; therefore, I may make mistakes or get it wrong." So now we also have others convinced and believing in our own limitations, which then strengthens this limiting belief further.

Have you ever had someone say to you, "Man, you look awful today", "You must be tired", "You have dark circles under your eyes", etc.? What did that do to your energy? More than likely, you experienced an energy discharge or drop, resulting in a deflation of your energy field. Such a drop can be felt either physically, emotionally, or mentally, or all of the above. That's because you bought into their reality about you, thereby making it stronger. But if you are consciously cancelling all negatives, you would not even consider their negative reality and would remain unaffected. Negative realities gain strength when we buy into them.

Do yourself a huge favour and avoid all negative "I am" statements. You can word things differently and bring about a win-win situation for all concerned.

One way you can do this is by following any true statement with a positive intent and outcome. For example: "I am having difficulty staying focused right now, and a little rest will replenish my energy, and I can then get back on top of things quickly." Or, "My energy is low, but it's getting stronger as the days goes on. My body is being restored to a state of great vitality, and I have great focus."

➤ Self-Sabotaging

Self-sabotage is a combination of thoughts, feelings, and actions that stop you from achieving your goals or succeeding in life. It's you creating obstacles that work against and ruin your own self-interests. Self-sabotage defies reason to the conscious mind yet makes perfect sense to the subconscious. We consciously set a short-term or long-term project or goal, decide what tasks need to be completed, and then either fall short of completing them or attract something that gets in the way or distracts us. This doesn't seem logical—unless you keep in mind that your subconscious is in control. Although the subconscious is all-powerful, it has humility. It will never force intent upon you; it would rather remain calm and lazy. Once you get in touch with how your subconscious mind functions and operates, you can begin to use the current it generates.

Some signs of self-sabotage:

- Doing silly things that you probably know better than to do, such as drinking too much the night before an exam or something important. Things like this set you up for failure or, at the least, a struggle.
- Doing things that are in direct opposition to what you want—such as your dreams, wishes, desires—and wondering why you do so.
- Listening to your negative inner dialogue or self-talk which never allows you to complete tasks or projects. In other words, not staying focused on your goal.
- Feeling like the whole world is against you. You feel frustrated, helpless, or depressed because you never seem to achieve your goals. Then it seems that even more things don your self-talk

The greatest investment you can offer yourself or anyone else is the ability to become self-aware. The nature of the subconscious to be under our conscious level of awareness, where it stores our self-sabotage patterns, is what makes it so tough to recognise them and deal with them. However, honest intent to become more interested in being self-aware will open up immense opportunity to discover the magic of your own being-ness and potential.

We are often completely unaware of how our actions (or our inaction) affect us and others in our lives. Sometimes we hear people say that they always have bad luck, that things never work out for them, or that they weren't born to be good at this or that. If we can wake up and realise that we have the ability to be in control of our reality and create our own situations, circumstances, and events, then we can begin to avoid these subconscious self-sabotage patterns and thus change this unsupportive internal dialogue. In order to do this, we need to bring our awareness and attention to a conscious level of clarity and begin to explore our feelings. Our feelings are very important, as they serve as a guidance system.

What's really happening when we sabotage ourselves? Subconsciously we may be frightened by a particular outcome, even though we say we want it. Take, for example, losing weight. Many overweight people have struggled for years, tried diet after diet, and haven't been able to lose the weight or keep it off. They berate themselves, push themselves harder, and try to force the weight off. But what's happening beneath the surface? Do they really want to lose their excess pounds? They may say they do, but what if their layers of fat are providing them with a sense of protection and security in an uncertain world? What if they feel the need to cover up and conceal themselves? Losing weight then becomes a threatening, frightening possibility. So they might sabotage their diet efforts in order to avoid feeling too vulnerable and exposed. Even though they say they want to lose weight (and even believe they do), they still might set themselves up for failure by sneaking food, skipping exercise, and then making a promise that they'll try harder the next day.

CHAPTER 10

Tools the Subconscious Mind Uses

➢ Imagination

The great Albert Einstein said, "Imagination is more important than knowledge." According to Merriam-Webster, the definition of imagination is "the act or power of forming a mental image of something not present to the senses or never before wholly perceived in reality".

If I were to ask you, "What is more powerful, your imagination or your willpower?" what would your answer be? Most people would say that willpower is more powerful. Actually, willpower is more dominantly used in general, but your imagination is far more powerful than your willpower. Whenever there is a conflict between the imagination and willpower, the imagination wins out every time. Just look at how many people have succeeded at diets and weight loss programmes and how many smokers have successfully permanently stopped smoking through willpower.

Willpower is likened to force, whereas imagination is likened to power. Within the imagination lie recipes for genius, and the constructive use of the imagination is a brilliant, totally overlooked gift. Intellectually I was aware of these facts; however, it wasn't until I had a personal experience with a client in a QHHT past-life regression session that opened up the true power and importance of the imagination that I really fully understood what everyone, including Einstein, had been talking about.

During QHHT hypnosis sessions, there is a procedure employed at the beginning of the session that utilises the imagination; it's a kind of warm-up of the mind, if you like, and a very simple technique; it is almost childlike in essence. It opens the door to the subconscious mind by bridging the conscious and subconscious in a subtle way.

Let's take a look at exactly how, once we have entered the subconscious mind, we can realise the important connection between the imagination and subconscious and how the two intimately interact together. In this context the imagination becomes a powerful presence, and you can begin to understand why imagination is so powerful and how it wins out whenever the conscious mind (willpower) and subconscious mind come into conflict.

Suppose a person—let's call him Alan—makes a conscious (willpower) decision to lose weight. But one day at the healthy buffet, someone offers Alan a cheesecake. Let's say Alan holds a belief in his conscious mind that cheesecakes are not healthy, but fattening, even though he enjoys (actually absolutely loves) the taste of cheesecakes. (The sense of taste is connected to imagination and the subconscious.) So Alan looks at the cheesecake and his inner dialogue says from a distance that cheesecakes are definitely fattening and unhealthy and certainly not one of the items he can allow himself to eat on his current diet. This is not a problem for Alan, though, because Alan is a strong man; he has willpower and mental strength to overcome small things like this. And Alan is determined to stick to his diet anyway. Alan can resist the temptation and pass on the cheesecake, even though it looks so good. Alan knows logically and rationally that if he wants to lose weight, then passing on the cheesecake is the rational, logical thing to do.

Alan's conscious mind knows what's best for him and his body, right? But, as if a magic genie has somehow conspired against him, Alan catches the scent of the lush, beautiful, creamy aroma radiating up from the fresh cheesecake. To add insult to injury and make things even more difficult for Alan, his wife, who is unaware of his internal struggle and who is also a cheesecake lover, is about to reach over to the buffet to pick up that last piece of cheesecake—*Alan's* cheesecake. Without hesitation,

Alan lunges for the cheesecake, grabs it, and then eats it, and with each bite he feels the nagging guilt from having cheated on his diet.

Why did this happen? Let me explain. The strength of Alan's emotional desire to eat the cheesecake, coupled with his imagination, which was stimulated by the scent and his senses, was greater than his desire to lose weight. In order to stop eating cheesecake, Alan would have to strengthen his desire and make a permanent change at the subconscious level so that his desire to lose weight would become stronger than his desire to eat cheesecake.

The emotional strength of our love (or fear) held in our subconscious minds will almost always topple and override rational thoughts and willpower in our conscious minds. When it comes to a battle of the minds, the subconscious mind will always win out. The subconscious doesn't mind at all if it is a slow and long battle; it's in no hurry. The key to having success in creating what we desire is to strike a bargain and convince the subconscious mind to go along with the decisions the conscious mind makes for us. One thing that the subconscious mind dislikes and does not enjoy is having something taken away from it. So one way to get around this is to soften this in some way. If we can substitute something else in its place and allow the subconscious to accept this as its new job and priority, the subconscious will be open and willing to agree, and then and only then can a successful and permanent change be achieved.

Just to ponder the grace and power of the imagination for a moment is really worthwhile. All the great concepts and inventions of mankind were initiated in the imagination first. A musician hears his song in his imagination before he puts it down on paper or plays it on a musical instrument. The same is true for fashion designers, dancers, and inventors. Every great poet and writer writes his stories in his imagination before putting them on paper. In fact, how can anyone be successful without his imagination?

The subconscious mind is a great friend to us and will do whatever we ask it to do if we ask it in the right way. The subconscious mind has only one priority, and that is to serve and protect us, period. Because the subconscious mind is activated by our imagination, there are no limits to what the subconscious will do for us. The only limitation is that the imagination is limited to what we believe we can imagine.

If we have a belief that it's not likely that we'll ever be healthy and wealthy, the subconscious scouts out and provides all the necessary requirements to bring this manifestation to fruition. In fact, the subconscious responds to every desire and imaginative thought we choose to entertain. Remember, as I stated earlier, the subconscious mind is literal. It does not judge or discriminate when it comes to thoughts and feelings. It will just as easily respond to a negative thought as it will to a positive thought or feeling. It responds to fearful thoughts as well as loving thoughts. Hence the importance of becoming aware and practising awareness of our inner dialogue, self-talk, thoughts, and feelings. This is a priceless skill worth taking the time to develop.

The subconscious mind is our friend and is always there for us. It never judges any of our thoughts or feelings or actions. Remember, the subconscious is the non-critical, non-analytical aspect of our mind, though we often judge ourselves with our conscious minds according to the belief systems we have created for ourselves. As our good friend, the subconscious is also extraordinarily protective of us. It will repress painful memories until we are ready to heal them.

➤ The Subconscious Mind Is the Home of Feeling

The subconscious is where the totality of our emotions and feelings are stored. Every emotion and feeling we experience is there. Whenever a familiar event occurs, it sends a ripple throughout our being-ness and is picked up by the subconscious and checked to see if it matches our previous experiences. The subconscious brings our thoughts and feelings to us instantly and automatically as events in our lives occur.

It is being realised more and more by individuals, groups, and even large corporations that there is some merit and value to the imagination. A fertile imagination is the fountain of all creative thinking. Most successful men and women in the higher salary brackets are there not because of hard physical work but because they used their active creative imaginations. One of the primary reasons most people are unsuccessful is that they never learned to use their imagination or they have a good imagination but it is supported by negative beliefs and thus creates negative experiences. We are all born with great imaginations. Notice children playing and observe how they use their unhindered imagination to solve problems and play. Most children live in a fantasy world for a number of years; it is a normal phase of personality development. Tell a child a bedtime story and note how you can effortlessly captivate his imagination. As the higher reasoning powers begin to rapidly set in, the child progresses into a world of realism. This is a critical development period as far as the imagination is concerned. Many young people almost completely quit using their imagination at this phase of their lives. Others (i.e. those interested in the arts) begin to make use of their imagination in a constructive way. Parents play an important role at this point. Encouragement is key to nourish the psyche. Some parents will recognise the importance of this and help guide their children into some creative outlet for their imagination to explore; unfortunately, though, the majority will completely miss it and may even stifle or inhibit the child's imagination.

Often the imagination flourishes during the later adolescent years until the individual has a collision with the hard, cruel world of adult reality. When this happens, many young people cease using their imagination generally for two reasons. Firstly, there is a stigma attached to people who use their imagination as being a little crazy or lazy. Also, if they have been hurt and disillusioned by the realities of the world, which most people have, they feel that if they allow their imagination to reign, it will create more experiences in which they will feel the same hurt and disillusionment.

➤ Components Used in Conjunction with the Imagination

The most creative portion of the subconscious mind is without doubt the imagination. Residing within the subconscious is the lush, fertile imagination. As I have touched upon already, the imagination is limited only by what you believe you can imagine. This then allows us the ability to create and manifest almost anything we want. The only thing that stops us from creating what we want is ourselves. We get in our own way. We even imagine our own blocks to what we want, and we are often not aware that we are doing this, as it operates on a subconscious level.

Imagination is the tool of geniuses, inventors, painters, artists, musicians, dancers, athletes, etc. The common thread amongst these successful people is that they all know how to use their imagination well. There is a flip side to this as well, and that is that if we allow our imaginations to be influenced by fear, doubt, uncertainty, and negative emotions, then undesirable results will be manifested. We have already discussed that what we focus upon will come into play. The subconscious will create undesirable negative results just as easily as it will create positive results. The key lies in how we use our imaginations and imagery in a way that serves us. Fortunately for us, the subconscious is open to listening to us and our instructions, and learning how the subconscious talks is a great way to learn how to communicate with it and get what we want. We are privileged to have freedom of choice, and we can choose which images we hold in our imaginations.

Following is a diagram of the boundaries of the parts of the mind that I refer to throughout this book. This may provide you with more clarity regarding how each part works and cooperates with each other part. It also makes clear how suggestions for change can be blocked by the critical filter (the conscious mind) and simultaneously displays how the critical factor can be bypassed to create change.

To the best of my knowledge, I believe this diagram was designed by Gerald Kein. Mr Kein is a very well known and highly respected hypnotherapist and the founder of the Omni Hypnosis Training Center in the USA. I like the way this diagram is designed, because it explains how the conscious and unconscious mind relates to the critical factor.

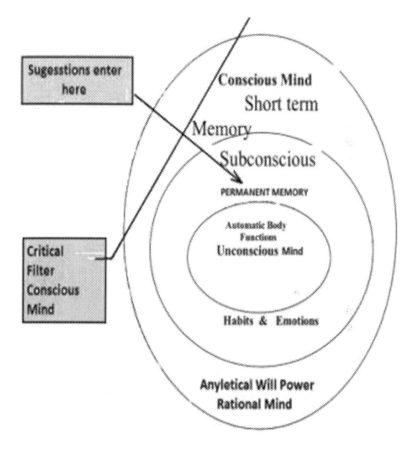

CHAPTER 11

Beliefs

You may not believe in a belief, or you may believe in a belief. Whether you believe or you don't believe, even this is a belief in itself. Henry Ford said it very well when he coined the phrase, "Whether you think you can or whether you think you can't, you're right." Here are two more of my favourite quotations relating to beliefs, both by Dr Wayne W. Dyer:

- "What you believe and conceive, you will receive."
- "You will see it when you believe it."

For the purpose of simplicity, we can divide beliefs into two categories. When we boil it down, there are only two types of beliefs that we need to know about: beliefs that work for us and beliefs that do not work for us. We call beliefs that work against us limiting beliefs, and we call beliefs that work for us positive beliefs. You have probably heard these terms before. So why do we have these two different styles of beliefs, and how are they formed?

Belief is a very powerful force that can make you or break you. In the previous chapters, I touched upon how information and data are received and accumulated via the subconscious mind and that we have been receiving and accumulating all of this data and information and storing all of it since our first breaths.

Once we reach an age where we can judge for ourselves, this information, which is energy, gets translated into what we call our thoughts and thinking. When these thoughts are repeated over and over, which they always are, energy begins to grow, forming clusters of thought energy. Thinking, or thought, is made up of energy, and energy is made up of vibration. These thought clusters are also clusters of vibrational energy. This vibrational energy (thought clusters) is then formed into beliefs.

These beliefs then also form clusters, and when they do, they form what we call our attitudes. Attitudes are clusters of thoughts and beliefs. The first thoughts that we probably had were transmitted to us telepathically or empathically by our parents and siblings. These are not really our original thoughts; they are borrowed thoughts, second-hand thoughts, thoughts that may or may not be true and may or may not be of any use to us.

This is a simplified explanation of the initial process of how our thoughts and beliefs begin to take shape during the early stages of life. When our parents, teachers, siblings, aunt, and uncles unconsciously began teaching us their beliefs, we had not yet developed our critical filter, so we accepted them early in childhood without any judgement. At that time it was all a natural learning process and we did not know any different, and in order to survive, we accepted it. As we grew older, we began to understand and accept that the fireplace was hot and would hurt us. We didn't have to place our hand in the fire to learn this.

This was an important step towards maturity and was a matter of necessity. These beliefs then developed into truths for us without much testing or searching to see if they would still work for us or, for that matter, if they ever did. We accepted these beliefs and took them for granted in a way and just accepted them as fact without questioning their validity.

As we matured, our parents and teachers continued to share their beliefs about how it all works, and we continued to accept most of what they said as truth. You see, it's much easier to accept the beliefs of those in authority when we are children; we learn very quickly that things go more smoothly when we do this. So as a young infant growing into young adulthood, we found ourselves unknowingly being subtly bombarded with the beliefs of our parents, siblings, aunts and uncles, extended families, Internet, TV, radio, media, books, magazines, employers, and so on.

It is important to realise and note that people's true beliefs are based upon their own personal experiences. The more such experiences a person has, the stronger his belief will be. Beliefs are developed from thoughts you had over and over until they became unconscious thoughts. And of course clusters of unconscious thoughts then form unconscious beliefs, which then form unconscious attitudes.

Regarding hypnotherapy and treatment, this knowledge on beliefs opens up the healing field so that we can penetrate deeply into the cause of an issue. In this area we are able to diagnose and pinpoint issues—whether mental illnesses, emotional illnesses, or physical illnesses—which are directly related to the health of an individual's beliefs.

Generally these diseases or illnesses occur because the current belief systems that an individual is holding and using are no longer serving the system and are therefore outdated. This renders the belief a no longer congruent and aligned service. The difficulty of recognising and rectifying this arises because these beliefs are under the conscious level of awareness; they are in the subconscious mind. It is very difficult to change or discard something that you are not even aware you have.

These beliefs may have been useful at a time in your life. Your beliefs are your momentum forward, which bring forth and manifest the results you see in your life. I heard this quotation somewhere, and I still remember it, because it is accurate: "What you believe and conceive you will receive." Because we don't realise we are being driven by these self-conscious beliefs, we never think to look closely at this and are thus then not able to verify that these beliefs are what are causing the problems. Usually it takes a disaster, a large setback, or a traumatic or even life-threatening situation in a person's life to get someone to stop and reassess his life. Obviously this is not the ideal way we would like to learn to discover how to do this; however, these types of scenarios are usually the only reason a person will finally stop to listen, take a look, and maybe consider something needs attention.

It is beautiful and comforting to know that our beliefs and belief systems are malleable and easy to change. And the journey to change one's beliefs is extremely rewarding. We can change the situation's circumstances and events in our lives instantly by changing our beliefs. The changes that occur on the outside are in exact proportion to the changes that occur on the inside. We must change on the inside before we can see the results occurring on the outside. Most people think that changing the outside will change the inside. However, this is akin to putting the cart before the horse. Our lives change as fast as we change our beliefs—no sooner, no later, no slower, no faster. It is in exact proportion.

There was a time when everybody believed that the world was flat, and this was the truth for them. However, that belief was changed overnight when it was discovered that the world was round. With this new, updated knowledge, it would have been ridiculous for people to still believe that the world was flat.

As I began the exciting study of examining my own my belief systems, I began to recognise the correlation between some of my current beliefs and the beliefs of my parents. I began to recognise where my parents' beliefs were holding them back from experiencing new possibilities in their lives. This did not happen through them not wanting to know; they just had not come into contact with the updated knowledge.

I was soon able to recognise where I had been holding myself back from experiencing more of what I wanted. This was an exciting discovery for me, as I instantly recognised the implications of where this could lead me. I had never noticed this prior, and I later discovered that there is terminology used for this in some systems of self-awareness training. This is known as a blind spot.

The more you begin to examine this area of your own life, the more you will begin to see these blind spots popping up here and there. This opens up more opportunities to discover old beliefs and let them go. It's a good feeling to experience these blind spots. Every time I recognise a blind spot, I know that I have just released an old belief and I know that a new possibility for me to discover more of myself and others has opened up.

➤ How Do Our Beliefs Limit Us?

Limiting beliefs are those beliefs which constrain us in some way. We're all driven, motivated, limited, empowered, and controlled by our beliefs. We have positive and negative beliefs, and these beliefs typically form and gain momentum over a long period of time. As mentioned in the previous chapter, from the day we pop out of mum, our subconscious minds are being effortlessly programmed like computers, resulting in our influences and our experiences. The formation of our world views and our accepted roles in life is a largely unconscious process for us.

It is common wisdom that if someone really believes he can do something, there is more of a possibility that he will be successful than if he doesn't believe he can do it. The act of believing in oneself contains a certain kind of magic that is difficult to explain in words. The act of believing aligns one with the power and cooperation of the universal force. In other words, there seems to be an invisible energy or source that supports and conspires to help people who hold a strong belief about something.

➤ Coincidences or Beliefs

Things that seem to be coincidences are never coincidences. There is always a reason why something has happened, even if we are not aware of what that may be at the time. We meet that right person at the right time right when we need to. We miss our train and catch the next train only to find out there is someone on the train we haven't seen for a long time. Or we meet someone that gives us some unexpected piece of information that we needed. These are positive examples of favourable occurrences.

However, coincidences that appear to be negative in nature can also arise. It has been documented and discovered that people who have similar illnesses or diseases, such as arthritis, heart disease, skin allergies, and even cancer, will often have very similar mental or emotional belief systems. They also tend to display a victim consciousness and engage in similar self-talk and inner dialogue, such as, "There's nothing I can do", "No one lives forever", "It's too late now", etc. Our beliefs about ourselves and what is possible in the world around us greatly impact our health and day-to-day effectiveness. We all live with the double-edged sword, having both beliefs that serve us and beliefs that limit us.

A number of studies have been conducted in this area, and one demonstrated the power of belief clearly in a revealing and enlightening study in which a group of children of average intelligence were divided at random into two equal groups.

The first group of children was assigned to a teacher who was told that all the children were gifted. The other group was given to a teacher who was told that the children were normal and slow learners. A year later, the two groups were retested for intelligence. Interestingly, and probably not surprisingly, the majority of the group identified as gifted performed better and scored higher than they had previously, while the majority of the group labelled normal and slow scored lower! It was discovered and identified that the teacher's beliefs about the students had an effect on their ability to learn.

There was another study done with one hundred cancer survivors (patients who had recovered and reversed their symptoms during a ten-year period). They were all interviewed about what they had done to achieve success to find out if there were any common threads between them. The interviews revealed that no one treatment method was outstanding as being more effective than any other. Some of the patients had taken the standard medical treatment of chemotherapy or radiation, some had used an alternative nutritional approach, others had followed a spiritual path, others concentrated on a psychological approach, and some did nothing at all.

What was discovered was that the only characteristic and common thread of the entire group was that they all believed that the approach they took was going to work.

Certainly these examples seem to indicate and demonstrate some power to support the notion that our beliefs can influence, shape, affect, or even determine our health, our relationships, our creativity, and the degree of our happiness and personal success. Yet if indeed our beliefs are so powerful a force in our lives, how do we get control of them so they don't control us, or at least so we can use them to benefit us? As we now know, most of our beliefs were collected and installed into our subconscious minds when we were children by parents, teachers, the Internet, social upbringing, magazines, pop stars, and the media before our critical filters had developed and we were aware of their impact or able to make choices about them.

This is why it is so important to become aware of our own self-talk, our inner dialogue, and begin to recognise what is useful and serving us and let go of or change old beliefs that may be limiting us. We can then reprogram the subconscious with new beliefs that can serve us positively and expand our potentials and possibilities beyond what we currently imagine possible.

CHAPTER 12

Creative Visualisation and Positive Thinking

Because the foundation of this book is really about opening up the subconscious mind, it would not be complete without touching on the subject of creative visualisation. Creative visualisation basically refers to the practice of using the imagination to affect the outer world and manifest things by focusing on certain thoughts, ideas, feelings, and emotions. It is said that just by being able to hold a certain picture or idea in the mind with a particular feeling for around thirty seconds is enough to start a new direction and momentum for new creative manifestations. If held for approximately sixty seconds, manifestation will occur on some level.

This technique of using one's imagination to visualise specific behaviours or events occurring in one's life and to utilise a combination of images and positive thinking is known as creative visualisation. Positive thinking on its own is really a mental attitude produced by one strong thought or clusters of thoughts, words, and images that are focused on growth, expansion and success. It is the tuning of a mental attitude that is cultured or customised to expect good and favourable results. A positive mental attitude anticipates a beneficial outcome fuelled by a momentum of healthy feelings of certainty towards whatever idea, situation, or event is desired. Whatever the mind expects builds up a momentum and an ability to recognise the synchronistic manifestations it produces. Most people generally call this coincidence. However, remember that coincidences are concepts, ideas, and thoughts that have been given momentum by you on the subconscious level and are now manifesting in reality for your conscious mind to observe. You may or may not be consciously aware that you are doing this, but you are. The more you become clear in your awareness, the more you will be able to recognise that you are creating these coincidences, and then, as you begin to realise you are creating these coincidences, this builds up a very positive feeling and excitement that perpetuates the whole process.

It is quite common to hear people say, "Think positive!" Although this subject is gaining more and more popularity these days, still not everyone accepts or believes in positive thinking. Amongst the people who accept it, not many know how to use it effectively to gain lasting results. Creative visualisation is one of the basic techniques underlying positive thinking and is being embraced as an effective method more frequently as we evolve. Again, the use of the imagination is involved here.

One of the most outstanding and well-known studies on creative visualisation techniques was done on sports. The Russians, who seem to experiment a lot with these ideas, were performing experiments and practising this concept a long time ago, and they began to use it in different areas and fields of life. A Russian scientist compared four groups of Olympic athletes in terms of their training schedules. Below is a summary of a post that I believe was posted by bksportswing/mind-power-and-sports.

- group 1-100% physical training
- group 2-75% physical training with 25% mental training
- group 3-50% physical training with 50% mental training
- group 4-25% physical training with 75% mental training

Interestingly, the studies revealed that group 4, with 75 per cent of their time devoted to mental training, performed the best. The Soviets discovered that mental images can act as a prelude to muscular impulses and begin to condition muscle responses and muscular activity.

To better understand and take advantage of the use of the imagination, it is just as important to know how to avoid using the imagination in the wrong way. Now I will note some of the mistakes we make in using our imaginations. Understanding these mistakes will help us shed light on areas where we may not be aware that we are making mistakes. Because we sometimes use our imaginations nearly twenty-four hours a day out of laziness, we can fall into certain habits of using imagination, thoughts, and feelings to produce negative results as well.

However, before we go any further, I'd like to share a perception or interpretation of the word "habit". A habit is only a habit when you don't know you have it. As soon as you know you have a habit, it is no longer a habit; it is a choice

Much of what is not working for us in our lives—the struggle and strains, pains, suffering, frustration, anguish, etc.—is largely created by our own unconscious negative use of our imaginations. The problem is that we just aren't conscious of it. Remember the blind spots we mentioned earlier. We can begin to become more conscious, and as we do that, we begin to become aware of our self-talk, our internal dialogue. (I will discuss internal dialogue and self-talk in the next chapter.)

The most crucial and oft overlooked ingredient for effective creative visualisation is the feelings. The imagination is the designer of the thoughts; your feelings are their fuel. Your feelings are your own personal guidance system. Although we experience many different feelings, textures of feelings, and mixtures of emotions, we basically operate from a foundation of two emotions: feeling good or feeling bad. All emotions will have an outcome of one other the other. However, in my experience I have found there to be three emotions. Emotions that feels good can be categorised as right, true, or positive. Those that feel bad fall under the category of negative, out of alignment, or false. Then there is a third emotion, the one that feels neither good nor bad. It sits in the middle, not really giving any clear indication of whether or not to make a choice in one particular direction or another. It's a feeling of uncertainty. I place this emotion into the category of false or negative. If an emotion that I feel is not clearly positive, I place it automatically into the category of negative and choose not to move in that particular direction if I desire a positive result. Yes, I know it sounds a little confusing, but it's really quite straightforward. If it feels good, make a choice to move in that direction; if it feels negative, avoid that direction; if it feels uncertain, stay where you are until you get a clearly positive feeling.

With this immediate feedback system of our emotions, we can tune into and focus on what feels good and focus on manifesting those results, and we can simultaneously avoid focusing on what we don't want to manifest. Your thoughts and feelings are what create the reality you experience. Believe it or not, we attract what we want based on how we are feeling. The world outside of you is a mirror of the inner you; the subconscious feelings and thoughts that you chronically think and feel all day long manifest the physical representation of what's happening on the world inside of you. Whatever you place your attention on is what grows and manifests into your daily living reality. In the same way, whatever you move your attention and focus away from fades and weakens.

The manifestation power of any mental image is determined by how often you imagine it. Each time you hold that particular thought or feeling and focus upon it, it strengthens, and the strength of the feelings or emotions associated with it will determine how quickly it will manifest. The secret is making your images, mental pictures, or mental movies feel real. Obviously it's important to make them feel believable to you so that you can achieve them. Then become conscious of your self-talk from this point forward. You will begin to notice as you become more conscious of this process that you can sometimes catch yourself thinking or feeling negatively. As you notice yourself saying something negative in your mind, you can stop your thought midstream. When you catch yourself in this habit, stop yourself and instead visualise and affirm the positive version of what you were feeling at the time.

CHAPTER 13

Stillness

Stillness of mind and breath form a bridge and a connection to our spirit. This is what most mediation techniques are based around. From this we can access a state of calm, clarity, peace, tranquillity, and self-restoration—a state of being that allows the body to heal and our energy to flow to where it is most needed in the body. Our thoughts slow down and can even cease, bringing us to a state called thoughtless awareness. This is the next step. Here we can replenish our drained energy and bring order to our scattered, agitated thoughts. This is a state where mind, emotions, and body can become strengthened and focused and less prone to being swayed or pulled into unwanted desires, thoughts, and images. This becomes a solid place where feelings, thoughts, and mind and body sensations can merge and integrate.

The beauty of stillness is that it does not have to be created; it is already innate. It's our source, and it is so natural to us that we may simply allow it to flow and come through as the energy it is, allowing it to move aside turbulence of the mind so that our internal dialogue can quiet down and settle. Just because you are being still and nothing much is active physically doesn't mean that being still is lazy and inactive. It is a state of active inactiveness. Once we cease fuelling the mind, ultimately turning down the volume on the internal dialogue, the mind decreases its mental activity as well and becomes receptive to the communications of the subconscious mind. This is where we begin to tap into our own knowledge, wisdom, creativity, healing ability, and well-being. There truly is a wealth of creativity, insight, and wisdom that lies within the psyches of us all.

During periods of stress we can become impulsive and more inclined to make poor or hasty decisions, which can lead to regretful, silly, and clumsy actions. Of course, having a clear, calm mind before making any important decisions is not a bad habit to have and will greatly improve the quality of our performances and the richness of our experiences. When we are under pressure and anxiety, we often feel that a decision is extremely urgent and need to consider first if this urgency is just a symptom of our distressed state. When we are feeling low or depressed, we often find that procrastination and loss of motivation get in the way of making decisions that do really need to be made. Accessing the meditative state of inner stillness can greatly improve these dysfunctional pitfalls.

➢ The Power of Being Present

Being present is not only about noticing what's happening now. It's more about becoming aware of your feeling, your presence, your being, your inner quietness, your stillness. As you put your attention on it now, you may notice you have to take your attention away from this moment to internalise it as you move from exterior mode to interior mode. The mind can be subtle, and we have built habits over time of focusing more on the future or on the past than on the present. But if you are super attentive to the present moment, you will notice that a kind of rhythmic dance forms between this moment and your mind.

The present is just like the stillness in that it has no resistance. This releases and frees us from harmful stress. In this state you are resisting nothing. You are not holding on to the past or fighting future possibilities. The body follows the mind, and the natural by-product of a peaceful mind is a resting body.

Resting in this state creates many benefits; one of those is the ability of the body to heal much faster than usual. The body's default is to heal; it naturally wants to do this in order to maintain balance. As soon as we are able to move out of the way of the natural healing default of the body, the faster we can heal. A person's appearance may greatly vary depending on how stressed or relaxed he is. People who look younger than they actually are tend to have more relaxed minds and healthier organs when practising stillness, meditation, or being in the present.

Returning to the present moment offers you an acceptance of the moment perfectly as it is without judgement. There is no wrong or right. There is only what is. As you begin to learn how to accept what is (your inner stillness), your stress levels will dramatically decrease, allowing you access to more of your natural energy to assert more control over your life events and circumstances.

It is perfect. You are perfect. It is complete. You are complete. There is nothing that needs fixing or adjusting. Acceptance in itself is a perfect recipe in itself; it's the key. If you can rest in the being-ness and knowledge that health and happiness are your birthright, your most natural way of being, then you can allow the natural rhythm of the body to bring about alignment and balance. The interesting thing is that the results calm us once we let go of the idea of trying to change or control things. For healthier results, focus your attention on enjoying the peace, love, and contentment that naturally happen when you are fully embracing this moment. In the stillness you can observe the content of your thoughts, and you will notice which time frame you are in at any given time. You will begin to notice how often your thoughts and feelings are focused on the past or the future.

As we covered earlier in the chapters of this book, these thoughts are riddled with judgements comparing the past or future to your present situation. It seems almost insane that people spend such little amounts of time in the present moment. Statistics show that most people contribute less than 1 per cent of their time to being fully present. The rest of the time, we drift in and out as our attention wanders in an aimless manner, lacking focus and power. Your mind may even seem to be out of control.

Your willingness to consciously activate your power of being in the present is key to experiencing a quality of life that surpasses the mundane and common human logic. You become enabled and empowered to see life and the world around you for what it truly is in such a way that it instils an indescribable sense of internal harmony, peace, and well-being that transcends all forms of common logic and widely held perceptions of possibility that the vast majority unconsciously choose to remain limited by.

Acceptance is a virtue that doesn't require any form of action in the physical sense of the word, yet neither is it a lazy state. It's an active, chosen way of being. Its reach is infinite in nature; it transcends ego and suspends polarity and duality, which in turn enables the flow of heartfelt desires to become "real and tangible".

Each and every experience we encounter in life, whether physical, financial, relational, emotional, or spiritual, doesn't find its root in doing, as the vast majority perceive, but in a chosen way of being.

This way of being is reflected and made real through the choices that you make for yourself at the causal level. More specifically, it is made real through the quality of consciousness that you choose for yourself.

There are no right or wrong ways of being; that is a judgement that is not possible whilst in a state of being. Only individual choices determine what you will experience in the various aspects of your life.

Those who discover acceptance and choose it as their predominant way of being find it such a pleasant state of ease to be in. It's a state in which things seem to flow with ease, as resistance has been let go of. Acceptance has myriad benefits. It will balance out your emotions, giving you a sense of emotional stability. It dissolves uncertainty, worry, doubt, fear, and anxiety, which in turn enables us to get back into alignment with our source of flow to align us. In this alignment we can consistently deliver more and more desirable outcomes. The more we find ourselves in alignment and can see the results of it, the more our enthusiasm is generated; this creates a positive spiral. Also, as we become aligned with this feeling, whenever we get out of alignment, we can notice it and then bring ourselves back into alignment again. As this process continues to become more familiar to us, the gaps between being out of alignment get shorter and we resume the alignment process more quickly and naturally.

We are human beings, not human doings; however, doing is physical, and this creates additional physical effects. Being is subtle; it is the underlying cause that permeates the physical realm and gives meaning to physical intents and actions. So the essence or quality of our chosen way of being affects the quality of our doing, which in turn impacts the quality of the tangible results that we receive, which in turn determines our individual circumstances, situations, events, or experiences, and even our physical appearances.

Notice that when you accept things you feel a certain ease permeate your being. It is our true nature to accept; it's one of the first things we experience when we enter into this life. Fear, anxiety, worry, etc. are all learned emotions, and anything that we have learned we can unlearn. Ironically, resistance, although it is often perceived as a method or means to avoid unpleasant and undesirable experiences, is in actuality the very choice that enables the unpleasant to become real in the first place. And therefore it persists only to serve us by drawing us more into the unpleasant situation that we are trying to avoid—precisely the polar opposite of we are looking for and want.

Put another way, our chosen way of being is the result of the quality of consciousness that we choose individually, and that way of being is made real based on this quality of consciousness. The quality of our consciousness serves as the seed of what we are being, which in turn is reflected in the tangible outcomes that our chosen way of being determines and harmonises with.

Obviously, both acceptance and resistance are choices available to us, but they are not always clearly recognised. These are choices made with awareness, and awareness is the perquisite of choosing wisely. Being aware and having some understanding as to how the processes unfold is going to work in your favour and be a great asset. Really anything less than this falls under the category of self-sabotage, because it is a form of self-sabotage.

To begin to tune into acceptance of everything around us, or what we can call "what is" is just as balanced as choosing to resist "what is". The beauty is that we have the choice. Therefore, make wise choices, because this will set the intent of what you want and what you manifesting into motion and flow.

The flow comes from the source; it is abundant and infinite in its nature. It never rests, and equally the process of attraction never rests. It's the nature of the universe to multiply and consistently supply an abundance of whatever we choose for ourselves. It is up to us what we choose.

➢ Let's Be Present

Discovering how to be present is one of the most important key contributing factors in my personal growth on all levels—physically, emotionally, mentally, and spiritually. The importance of the power and asset of learning how to become present cannot be emphasised enough. We hear it all the time from the gurus, masters, motivational speakers, etc. But when you finally feel it and understand it for yourself in a state of presence, you really get what they have all been talking about. When you have a clear mind, you are decisive, you know what you want, you perform your best, and you have an inner sense of confidence that runs deep.

One of the fastest ways—and possibly the only way—to engage the brain in changing any behaviour or emotion is to stay in the present moment. To help myself become more present, I came up with this phrase: "Be present of being present." I continually reminded myself to be present of being present. This has been very helpful in assisting me to stay in the present more consistently. I was able to place myself outside myself, in a way, so that I could monitor my state more easily. I practise being in the present every day, and whenever I catch myself not in the present moment, I bring myself back to the present moment immediately.

It is my belief that we are infinite conscious awareness. We are not naturally separate from awareness; it is our source. But we can be distracted by our desires or other things, and thus we can be drawn into the future or into the past, which takes our attention away from the present. Acceptance is the opposite to judgement. Judgement is a fear-based awareness which usually leads to the formation of negative emotions, such as frustration, inferiority, or even a sense of unworthiness. It's not uncommon for these negative emotions to then lead towards some form of anger or resentment. Unexpressed resentment will lead to anger, and anger can often spiral into conflict. Nevertheless, all of these feelings and emotions are feelings of separation and disconnection.

Our bodies and our minds are an integrated and interactive system that works together. It's impossible to completely separate the two. They are so interconnected that if we're thinking or worried about something, our bodies will respond to our worried thoughts and produce chemical changes within our systems. Everyone experiences stress differently, but stress and worry often cause our bodies to become tense and nervous, causing us to breathe in low, shallow breaths.

Shallow breathing effects a person's behaviour and how he acts on many levels. Low oxygen levels lead to nervousness, sluggishness, irritability, a lack of energy, fatigue, and depression. An individual's personality can really be affected by this. Shallow breathing also reduces the amount of oxygen taken into the body. The brain relies upon oxygen to function, and when the supply becomes low, the brain cannot operate at full capacity. This side effect manifests itself in many ways, such as memory loss, lack of concentration, and increased time to accomplish simple tasks.

It is stated that If you are one of those people who have formed the habit of under-breathing all day and you have a high salt intake, your kidneys may be less effective at getting rid of that salt. High blood pressure affects about one of every five adults these days. Blood pressure allows blood to flow and deliver oxygen and food to the body. While anyone can get high blood pressure, people who are overweight and inactive and eat too much salt are at higher risk.

CHAPTER 14

Conscious Breathing

One of the first things that I do when I meet my clients for the first time and we have completed our pre-talk and we are comfortably sitting down together, just prior to beginning the induction, is ask them to take a few deep breaths while I carefully watch how they breathe.

Surprisingly, only about one out of ten people actually breathes correctly. And generally the people who breathe correctly are familiar with some form of healing, sports, or meditation techniques. So, for those who breathe incorrectly, I spend a few minutes with them, helping them to become conscious of how they should breathe and how they were breathing incorrectly. I then help them to correct their breathing, and they do a few breaths with my guidance as I correct the breathing along the way. I often get a clear and distinct feeling that this is probably the first time they have breathed properly for a long time, possibly even since childhood.

Once I've corrected their breathing, it is very common for my clients to look surprised at how much better they feel from just taking a few proper deep breaths. Our breathing is very important, and based on my experience with my clients, it is often overlooked.

When we can focus on slow conscious breathing, we are able to absorb much more oxygen. Of course we know that a shortage of oxygen to the brain will increase irritability and tiredness, resulting in a lack of energy. Concentration is affected, and of course productivity is reduced.

The more oxygen our body has access to, the more beneficial our mind/ body chemistry becomes. But why don't we take much notice of this?

Through my experience as a hypnotherapist, I generally find that people are breathing too shallow. Taking longer to breathe out enables you to take in more oxygen on the next breath.

Breathing is an unconscious activity of the body. Look at a baby breathing, and you will see that children naturally breathe in the right way. Conscious breathing can help provide a tool to manage the daily stresses of life. Along with the imagination, the breath is also the bridge between the mind, the body, and the spirit. The imagination is more a bridge of the subconscious mind and body; however, these two principles in tandem are powerful keys to well-being. There is a breathing rhythm associated with all the physical and psychological states of the body and mind. There is a breath for passion, a breath for anger, a breath for fear, a breath for joy, a breath for sorrow, and a breath for happiness.

We may not be able to control external stressors, but we can learn to control our reactions to them and reduce their effects on our lives by being in a more accepting state of being. This state of being can be induced, deepened, and prolonged by combining conscious breathing with stillness of mind. Sitting in a comfortable position or even lying down is also okay; do whatever is comfortable for you. Becoming aware of your breathing for a few minutes will help still the mind, and then you can become aware of your thoughts slowing down. This simple and basic meditation can have a very positive and even profound effect on your health and well-being.

CHAPTER 15

De-Hypnotisation

One of the main issues and problems society is facing and has yet to realise is that they have already been hypnotised. You've already been hypnotised whether or not you're aware that you have been hypnotised.

As I previously mentioned, we have been hypnotised right from the moment we were born (some believe this occurs even before we are born, when we are still in the womb). So let's start from the day we are born. We are guided by our parents, grandparents, peers, teachers, television and various other avenues. The hypnosis runs very subtly within us. One of the most powerful ways we are hypnotised is through culture. I believe that culture does serve a positive nurturing purpose as a guiding style, tool, or even mechanism through the early years of our lives. However, if an individual does not begin to use his own knowledge and wisdom, his cultural upbringing becomes a dangerous trap and can be quite detrimental to his creativity and his direction and happiness in life.

I see culture as being kind of like training wheels on a bicycle. Once you begin to learn to ride a bicycle, the training wheels are very helpful and sometimes necessary in stabilising and guiding you until you get your balance and you can ride the bicycle with your own balance and creativity. However, once you have gained your balance and confidence and you can ride the bicycle yourself, there is no longer any need for the training wheels, and they can come off. Once the training wheels are off, the rider can experience an expanded sense of freedom and more fully enjoy riding a bicycle. He can turn corners more easily and feel the momentum and speed more easily; he also gains a sense of confidence that he's now balancing the bicycle himself. In a way, learning to ride a bicycle is quite an achievement and is probably one of the first experiences of freedom and independence a child feels. I know it was for me.

Culture is just like those training wheels. Once you reach a certain age, the culture has guided you and given you a sense of wisdom and direction, and it is time to begin to think for yourself and think on your own two feet, developing your independent skills. However, I have observed that certain cultures can be so strongly ingrained in people through beliefs and belief systems that people become attached to the culture and attached to the ways of the culture. This can be a limitation; it is similar to leaving training wheels on a bicycle.

If we take a quick look at what culture is made up of, we can basically discover, if we simplify it, that culture is knowledge that has been passed down from one generation to another generation on the basis of trial and error and the beliefs of that particular cultural system. We could say that the people who came before us tried out different things and different ways of doing things and discovered that some of these things worked and some of these things didn't work. They then passed that information on to us in order to save us the effort, time, and pain of trying to figure out what works and what doesn't. It is highly likely that this was also the procedure of the predecessors of that generation.

There are several things that can be fallible in following this procedure. Firstly, the ways of doing things in the previous generations may have worked very well at that point in time and served a great purpose; however, as humans evolve and technology evolves, some of these ways fall behind the times and are superseded by more efficient methods and ways of doing things.

Secondly, and I think more importantly, believing in these old methods and following them can make a person lazy by allowing him to rely upon other people's work and discoveries. This is actually contrary to our nature; we are creative beings. We need to be creative; we need to keep on using our creative abilities to remain healthy, to keep our mind functioning clearly, and to feel a sense of satisfaction, a sense of freedom of expression, a sense of achievement. This also builds our self-confidence. Whilst it's a great feeling to have someone show you how to do something and feel supportive, there's nothing like that wonderful feeling of self-satisfaction when you create something from nothing and realise that it's a piece of genius that came from within you and you did it all by yourself. This is one of the keys to building self-esteem.

The current standard education system usually does not support this type of creativity and individualism, and the children become starved of their own source of self-esteem from an early age. I believe that this is one of the reasons that children become very frustrated and restless at school. We are born creators, and creative expression is necessary for our health and growth.

So as we grow up, all of this conditioning that we receive from the people around us, our environment, our friends and teachers, etc., is something that we need to become aware of and begin to sort out if we want to begin to know ourselves more. By an eliminatory process, we can begin to discover, release, and let go of all of those beliefs and attitudes that are not really ours that we borrowed or embraced in the past. Using these second-hand and borrowed belief systems has actually unknowingly placed us into a state of hypnosis. So we need to de-hypnotise ourselves to clean out the conscious and subconscious mind before we can see and discover who and what we really are and our true potentials and capabilities. We can begin to do this with the tool of awareness. Becoming aware of these thoughts, feelings, and beliefs within ourselves gives us the opportunity and the choice to take a look and examine them closely to see if they truly work for us and are in alignment with our truth or are out of alignment with our truth and do not work for us.

This simple process and method is an incredibly liberating experience in itself. It begins to free us and loosen us up mentally, emotionally, and physically. This has a relaxing and soothing effect on our minds, emotions, and bodies and perpetuates a sense and state of peace and relaxation. This freeing up, the sense of loosening and relaxation, is then able to begin to seep in between the cracks of the crumbling walls of the rigid thoughts, attitudes, and belief systems that have been built up over time. As this process continues, more and more clarity is experienced. We are able to proceed even deeper through the layers, sifting out and releasing and letting go of all of the stuff that is not working for us. It is a kind of mental and emotional housecleaning, if you like.

It's really important for us to begin to cleanse our minds in this way so that we can then begin to establish a connection with our true source of creativity and first-hand knowledge. This is when life for me began to become very exciting. I was able to recognise that there is infinite possibility and that anything that we want for ourselves is limited only by our imaginations. I found that we can create whatever we would like; this certainly is an exciting proposition. And since this time I have been manifesting and creating more and more of the things that I love in my life through this system.

I meet many people every day in my daily activities, and I notice how many people are caught up and entrapped in their minds. Sometimes during the course of our conversations, I will bring their attention back to their feelings. I often observe their faces as they enter and reconnect with their feelings for a moment, and it's as though they had almost forgotten about their feelings. It appears that the mind has become much overused, and for some it has obviously become a device to escape from the reality of life.